SBN 361 03901 8
Copyright © 1977 Darrell Waters Limited
"Five on a Hike Together" first published by
Hodder and Stoughton Limited in 1951
Published 1977 by Purnell Books, Berkshire House,
Queen Street, Maidenhead, Berkshire
Made and printed in Great Britain by
Purnell and Sons Limited, Paulton (Bristol)
and London

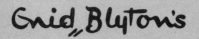

Enid Blyton's

FAMOUS FIVE

Go on a hike together

Annual

Purnell

Contents

Identikit

Julian

Julian is Anne and Dick's older brother. He is the most practical of the Five and is really their leader. He is very good at sport and is an expert swimmer.

George

George is Anne, Julian and Dick's cousin. She and Anne are at school together. The name George is short for Georgina. In her heart of hearts she would rather be a boy, and her impetuous ways and quick temper get her into all sorts of scrapes. She always ends up laughing, however, as she is really a very good-natured girl.

Anne
Anne is Julian and Dick's sister. She is gentler and more timid than her brothers and her cousin George. She is the cautious one and sometimes stops the others being too reckless.

Timmy
Timmy is a very important member of the Famous Five. He belongs to George, and lives in kennels at her school during term-time, but is beloved by all the children and *always* accompanies them on their adventures.

Dick
Dick is Anne and Julian's brother. He and Julian are at the same school and are close friends, although Julian, being the elder of the two, normally takes the lead in their adventures.

Introduction

Five Go on a Hike Together Annual is a brand new annual about Enid Blyton's popular characters—the Famous Five. But it's an annual with a big difference, because it contains, complete, the title story—chosen from the best of the Five's adventures. Some of the story is in the form of a picture strip and some of it is straightforward narrative, illustrated in black and white. As well as this exciting adventure story, you will find the annual packed with all sorts of articles, features and projects, some in full colour, and all of them directly or indirectly linked to the adventures of the Five.

You'll find an article on Youth Hostelling, how to make a kite, features on foxes and badgers, information on camping equipment, and lots of interesting tips, advice and things to do for everyone who enjoys action and the outdoor life.

Watch out for the next Famous Five Annual, and its companion, The Secret Seven Annual.

Chapter 1

A Letter from Julian

'ANNE!' shouted George, running after her cousin as she went along to her classroom. 'Anne! I've just been down to the letterboard and there's a letter from your brother Julian. I've brought it for you.'

Anne stopped. 'Oh thanks,' she said. 'What *can* Julian want? He only wrote a few days ago – it's most extraordinary for him to write again so soon. It must be something important.'

'Well, open it and see,' said George. 'Hurry up – I've got a maths class to go to.'

Anne ripped open the envelope. She pulled out a sheet of notepaper and read it quickly. She looked up at George, her eyes shining.

'George! Julian and Dick have got a few days off at our half-term week-end! Somebody's won a wonderful scholarship or something, and the boys have got two days tacked on to a week-end to celebrate! They want us to join them in a hike, and all go off together.'

'What a glorious idea!' said George. 'Good old Julian. I bet he thought of that. Let's read the letter, Anne.'

But before she could read it a mistress came along. 'Georgina! You should be in class – and you too, Anne.'

George scowled. She hated to be called by her full name. She went off without a word. Anne tucked the letter into her pocket and rushed off joyfully. Half-term with her brothers, Julian and Dick, and with George and Timmy the dog. Could anything be better?

She and George talked about it again after morning school. 'We get from Friday morning till Tuesday,' said George. 'The boys are getting the same. What luck! They don't usually have a half-term in the winter term.'

'They can't go home because the painters are in our house,' said Anne. 'That's why I was going home with you, of course. But I'm sure your mother won't mind if we go off with the boys. Your father never likes us in the middle of the term.'

'No, he doesn't,' said George. 'He's always deep in the middle of some wonderful idea, and he hates to be disturbed. It will suit everyone if we go off on a hike.'

'Julian says he will telephone us tonight and arrange every-thing,' said Anne. 'I hope it will be a nice fine week-end. It will still be October, so there's a chance of a bit of warm sunshine.'

'The woods will be beautiful,' said George. 'And won't Timmy enjoy himself! Let's go and tell him the news.'

The boarding-school that the two girls were at was one that allowed the children to bring their own pets to school. There were kennels down in the yard for various dogs, and Timmy lived there during term-time. The two girls went to get him.

He heard their footsteps at once and began to bark

He flung himself on the two girls, licking and pawing

9

excitedly. He scraped at the gate of the kennel yard, wishing for the thousandth time that he could find out how to open it.

He flung himself on the two girls, licking and pawing and barking.

'Silly dog. Mad dog!' said George, and thumped his back affectionately. 'Listen, Tim – we're going off for the week-end with Julian and Dick! What do you think of that? We're going on a hike, so you'll love it. All through the woods and up the hills and goodness knows where!'

Timmy seemed to understand every word. He cocked up his ears, put his head on one side and listened intently while George was speaking.

'Woof,' he said, at the end, as if he approved thoroughly. Then off he went with the girls for his walk, his plumy tail wagging happily. He didn't like term-time nearly as much as the holidays – but he was quite prepared to put up with kennel life so long as he could be near his beloved George.

Julian rang up that night as he had promised. He had got everything planned already. Anne listened, thrilled.

'It sounds super,' she said. 'Yes – we can meet where you say, and we'll be there as near as we can on time. Anyway, we can wait about if you others aren't there. Yes – we'll bring the things you say. Oh Julian, won't it be fun!'

'What's he say?' asked George impatiently when at last Anne put the receiver down. 'You might have let me have a word with Julian. I wanted to tell him all about Timmy.'

'He doesn't want to waste an expensive telephone call listening to you raving about Timmy,'

said Anne. 'He asked how he was and I said "fine", and that's all he wanted to know about Tim. He's made all the arrangements. I'll tell you what they are.'

The girls went off to a corner of their common-room and sat down. Timmy was there too. He was allowed in at certain times, and so were three other dogs belonging to the girls. Each dog behaved well – he knew that if he didn't he would be taken back to the kennels at once!

'Julian says that he and Dick can get off immediately after breakfast,' said Anne. 'So can we, so that's all right. He says we've got to take very little with us – just night-things, tooth-brush, hair-brush and flannel and a rolled-up mac. And any biscuits or chocolate we can buy. Have you any money left?'

'A bit,' said George. 'Not much. Enough to buy a few bars of chocolate, I think. Anyway,

you've got all the biscuits your mother sent last week. We can take some of those.'

'Yes. And the barley sugar one of my aunts sent,' said Anne. 'But Julian says we're not to take much because this is to be a proper hike, and we'll get tired if we have to carry a heavy load. Oh, he said put in two pairs of extra socks.'

'Right,' said George, and she patted Timmy who was lying close beside her. 'There's going to be a long walky-walk, Tim. Won't you love that!'

Timmy grunted comfortably. He wondered if there would be any rabbits on the walk. A walk wasn't really exciting unless there were rabbits all over the place. Timmy thought it was a pity that rabbits were allowed to live down holes. They always disappeared most unfairly just when he had nearly caught one!

Anne and George went to see

The girls went off to a corner of their common-room and sat down

their house-mistress to tell her that they were not going to Kirrin Cottage after all, but were going walking.

'My brother says he has written to you,' said Anne. 'So you'll know all about it tomorrow, Miss Peters. And George's mother will be writing too. We can go, can't we?'

'Oh, yes – it will be a lovely half-term for you!' said Miss Peters. 'Especially if this sunny weather lasts. Where are you going?'

'Over the moors,' said Anne. 'In the very loneliest, most deserted parts that Julian can find! We might see deer and wild

ponies and perhaps even a few badgers. We shall walk and walk.'

'But where will you sleep if the parts you are going to are so very lonely?' asked Miss Peters.

'Oh, Julian is arranging all that,' said George. 'He's been looking up little inns and farm-houses on the map, and we shall make for those at night. It will be too cold to sleep out of doors.'

'It certainly will!' said Miss Peters. 'Well don't get into trouble, that's all. I know what you five are when you get together. I imagine Timmy is going with you too?'

'Of *course*!' said George. 'I wouldn't go if he didn't go! I couldn't leave him here alone.'

The two girls got their things ready as Friday came near. The biscuits were taken out of the tin and put into paper bags. The barley sugar was put into a bag too, and the bars of chocolate.

Both girls had rucksacks with straps for their shoulders. They packed and repacked them several times. One by one more and more things were added. Anne felt she must take a book to read. George said they must each take a torch with a new battery.

'And what about biscuits for Timmy?' she said. 'I simply must take something for him. He'd like a bone too – a big one that he can chew and chew and that I can put back into the bag for another time.'

'Well, let me carry all the biscuits and chocolate then if you're going to put a smelly old bone into your bag,' said Anne. 'I don't see why you want to take *anything* for Timmy – he can always have something to eat when we do – wherever we have a meal.'

George decided not to take the

bone. She had fetched one from his kennel, and it certainly was big and heavy, and equally certainly it was smelly. She took it back to the kennel again, Timmy following her rather puzzled. Why keep carrying his bone here and there? He didn't approve at all.

It seemed a long time till Friday, but at last it came. Both girls woke up very early indeed. George was out in the kennels before breakfast, brushing and combing Timmy to make him look spruce and tidy for Julian and Dick. He knew it was the day they were to set off and he was as excited as the two girls.

'We'd better eat a good breakfast,' said Anne. 'We might have to wait some time before our next meal. Let's slip off immediately after breakfast. It's lovely to feel free of school and bells and time-tables – but I shan't feel *really* free till I'm outside the school grounds!'

They ate an enormous breakfast though really they were too excited to want much. Then they got their rucksacks, ready-packed the night before, said goodbye to Miss Peters, and went to fetch Timmy.

He was waiting impatiently for them, and barked madly when they came near. In a trice he was out of his kennel-yard and capering round them, almost tripping them up.

'Good-bye, Anne and George!' yelled one of their friends. 'Have a good time on your hike – and it's no good coming back on Tuesday and telling us you've had one of your usual hair-raising adventures, because we just shan't believe it!'

'Woof,' said Timmy. 'Woof, woof!' Which meant that *he* was going to have adventures with hundreds of rabbits, anyway!

HAPPY CAMPING!

CAMPING is one of the most exciting and enjoyable activities any boy or girl could undertake. At least, it *could* be. Whether or not it proves a success depends very largely on what preparations you make. Take a tip from Julian. Whenever the Five decided to go camping he made sure that nothing was forgotten or overlooked before they set off. It's no fun to find yourself without a torch or a mac on a wild and stormy night, miles from anywhere!

Make a list of everything you think you will need. Apart from the obvious things such as change of clothes, sleeping kit, cooking utensils and so on, don't forget a needle and thread (in case you have a 'ripping' time!), a few safety pins, pencil and paper, a torch with a spare bulb and battery if possible, and – very important – a small first-aid kit which includes small bandages, an antiseptic, adhesive dressings, cotton wool and a pair of scissors.

Whilst thinking of first-aid matters, be ready for the most likely 'accident – a bee or a wasp sting. The two stings are different and should be treated differently. In the case of a bee sting, remove the barbed sting as quickly as possible with a needle, a pair of tweezers, or a split match. Dab the spot freely with a solution of ammonia. A wasp sting is an alkali so you should treat it with lemon juice or vinegar, which are acids. Make a note of this in case of emergency. But if a bee or wasp sting seems to be having serious effects, see a doctor without delay.

Always remember that tent material can easily catch fire. If you *must* use a candle for lighting, be sure to put it in a jam jar so that the flame is below the top of the jar. Better still, rig up an electric light from a battery, or make do with your torch. Also, be sure to keep your camp fire well clear of your tent – a flying spark may leave you without a roof over your head! If possible, see that your fire is to the windward side of the tent.

Rain or heavy dew will cause the tent canvas and the guy lines to tighten. Never retire for the night with the guy lines taut, otherwise there will be no slack to allow for shrinkage. Something has to give, and that something will be the tent pegs. They may be pulled right out of the ground and you will wake in the middle of the night to find the tent on top of you!

Another point to remember is never to touch the inside of the tent canvas during wet weather. The heat from your hand will cause the material to 'spring a leak' and water will seep through at this point. The best thing to do is to run your finger down from the leak to the bottom of the tent. The seeping water will follow this course instead of dripping on your bedding. Fortunately, these leaks will right themselves as the canvas dries.

In Britain, the wind and rain come mostly from the west or south-west, so when setting up your tent it is a good plan to have the tent door facing east or north.

Always ask permission of the owner of the land before you pitch your tent. It is the people who don't who spoil things for others.

Choose the site for your tent carefully. It may seem exciting to choose a spot close to a river or lake, but you will be in danger of massed attack by midges! And there are three good reasons why it is unwise to pitch your tent under a tree. A tree may be struck by lightning, it may shed a limb without warning (especially in view of Dutch elm disease), and raindrops from a leafy tree can cause you more trouble than a rainstorm in the open.

Make sure you know the Country Code and follow its advice.

If you want to know more about the joys and technicalities of camping, your local library is sure to have lots of helpful books on the subject. Here's wishing all Famous Five fans happy camping!

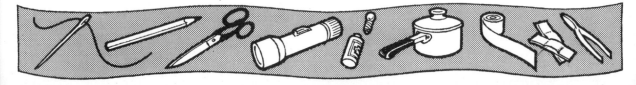

Chapter 2

Setting Off

JULIAN and Dick were also on their way, very pleased to have such an unexpectedly long week-end.

'I never liked Willis or Johnson much,' said Dick, as they walked out of the school grounds. 'Awful swotters they were – never had any time for games or fun. But I take my hat off to them today! Because of their swotting they've won medals and scholarships and goodness knows what – and we've got a week-end off in celebration! Good old Willis and Johnson!'

'Hear, hear,' said Dick. 'But I bet they'll sit in a corner with their books all the week-end – they won't know if it's a brilliant day like this, or pouring with rain like yesterday! Poor mutts!'

'They'd hate to go off on a hike,' said Julian. 'It would be utter misery to them. Do you remember how awful Johnson was at rugger? He never knew which goal he was playing against – always ran the wrong way!'

'Yes. But he must have got terrific brains,' said Dick. 'Why are we talking about Willis and Johnson? I can think of plenty of more interesting things – Anne and George, for instance – and old Tim. I hope they'll manage to get off in time all right.'

Julian had carefully looked up a large-scale map of the moors that lay between the two schools that he and the girls went to. They were vast stretches of lonely heathery land, dotted with farms here and there, with a few small cottages, and some inns.

'We'll keep right off the main roads, and the second and third-grades,' he said. 'We'll take the little lanes and paths. I wonder what Timmy will say if we see deer. He'll wonder what in the world they are!'

'He'll only be interested in rabbits,' said Dick. 'I hope he's not as fast as he was last hols. I think we must have given him too many ice-creams and too much chocolate!'

'Well, he won't get that in term-time!' said Julian. 'The girls don't get as much pocket money as we do. Buck up – there's the bus!'

They ran for the little country bus that rumbled along the country lanes, taking people to market, or to the tiny villages that lay here and there tucked away in the moor. It stopped most obligingly for them, and they leapt in.

'Ha! Running away from school?' said the conductor. 'Have to report you, you know!'

'Very funny,' said Julian, bored at this joke, which the conductor produced regularly every time a boy got on board with a rucksack over his shoulders.

They had to get out at the next village and cut across country to get to another bus-route. They managed to catch a bus there easily and settled down comfortably in their seats. It was half an hour's run from there to where they had planned to meet the girls.

'Here you are, young sirs,' called the conductor, as the bus ran into a village. It had a wide green on which geese cackled, and a small pond for ducks. 'You wanted Pippin Village, didn't you? We don't go any farther – we just turn round and go back.'

'Thanks,' said the boys and got out. 'Now – are the girls here or not?' said Julian. 'They have to walk from a tiny railway station about two miles away.'

They were not there. Julian and Dick went to have a drink of orangeade at the village store. They had hardly finished when they saw the two girls looking in at the door.

'Julian! Dick! We guessed you'd be eating or drinking!' said Anne, and she rushed at her brothers. 'We came as quickly as we could. The engine broke down – it was such a funny little train! All the passengers got out and advised the engine-driver what to do!'

'Hallo!' said Julian, and gave Anne a hug. He was very fond of his young sister. 'Hallo, George! My, you've grown fat, haven't you?'

'I have not,' said George, indignantly. 'And Timmy isn't fat either, so don't tell him he is.'

'Julian's pulling your leg as usual,' said Dick, giving George a friendly slap on the back. 'All the same, you've grown a bit – you'll soon be as tall as I am. Hallo, Timmy! Good dog! Tongue as wet as usual? Yes, it is! I never knew a dog with a wetter tongue than yours!'

Timmy went nearly mad with joy at being with all four of his friends. He leapt round them, barking, wagging his long tail and sending a pile of tins crashing to the floor in his delight.

'Now, now!' said the shop-woman, emerging from a dark little room at the back. 'Take that dog out. He's gone mad!'

'Don't you girls want a drink of ginger-beer or something?' asked Julian, getting hold of Timmy's collar. 'You'd better, because we don't want to have to carry heavy bottles of drink-ables with us.'

'Where are we going to set off to?' asked George. 'Yes, I'd like ginger-beer please. Get down, Timmy. Anyone would think you'd been away from Julian and Dick for at least ten years!'

'It probably does seem like ten years to him,' said Anne. 'I say – are those sandwiches?'

She pointed to a ledge at the back of the counter. There was a little pile of sandwiches there, looking most appetizing.

'Yes, they're sandwiches, Miss,' said the shop-woman, opening two bottles of ginger-beer. 'I've made them for my son who works over at Blackbush Farm – he'll be in for them soon.'

'I suppose you couldn't make *us* some, could you?' asked Julian. 'We wouldn't need to bother about trying to get to some village at lunch time then. They look jolly good.'

'Yes. I can make you all you want,' said the shop-woman, putting two glasses down in front of the girls. 'What do you want – cheese, egg, ham or pork?'

'Well – we'd like some of all of those,' said Julian. 'The bread looks so nice too.'

'I make it myself,' said the woman, pleased. 'All right – I'll go and make you some. You tell me if anyone comes into the shop while I'm gone.'

She disappeared. 'That's good,' said Julian. 'If she makes plenty of those we can avoid villages all the day and have a really good day of exploration – treading where no foot has trod before and all that!'

'How many can you manage each?' asked the woman, suddenly reappearing. 'My son, he has six.'

'Well – could you manage eight sandwiches for each of us?' said Julian. The woman looked astonished. 'It's to last us all day,' he explained, and she nodded and disappeared again.

'That's a nice little sum for her,' said Anne. 'Eight sandwiches each, making sixteen rounds of bread – for four people!'

'Well, let's hope she's got a bread-cutting machine!' said Dick. 'Or we'll be here for keeps! Hallo – who's this?'

A tall man appeared at the entrance of the shop, a bicycle in his hand. 'Ma!' he called.

The children guessed who he was at once – the son who worked over at Blackbush Farm. He had come for his sandwiches!

'Your mother is hard at work cutting sixty-four rounds of bread,' said Dick. 'Shall I get her for you?'

'No. I'm in a hurry,' said the man, and he set his bicycle by the door, came in, reached over the counter for his sandwiches and then went back to his bicycle.

'Tell my mother I've been in,' he said. 'And you might tell her I'll be late home today – got to take some stuff to the prison.'

He was off at once, sailing away down the road on his bicycle. The old woman suddenly came in, a knife in one hand, a loaf in the other.

'Did I hear Jim?' she said. 'Oh yes – he's got his sandwiches. You should have told me he was in!'

'He said he was in a hurry,' explained Julian. 'And he said we were to tell you he'd be late today because he had to take some stuff to the prison.'

'I've got another son there,' said the woman. The four looked at her. Did she mean he was a prisoner? And what prison?

She guessed their thoughts and smiled. 'Oh, my Tom isn't a prisoner!' she said. 'He's a warder – a fine fellow. Not a nice job there though – I'm always afraid of those men in prison – a fierce lot, a bad lot!'

'Yes – I've heard there is a big prison on this moor,' said Julian. 'It's marked on our map, too. We're not going near it, of course.'

'No. Don't you take the girls near there,' said the woman, disappearing again. 'If I don't get on with your sandwiches you'll not have them before tomorrow morning.'

Only one customer came in while the children were waiting – a solemn old man smoking a clay pipe. He looked round the shop, couldn't see the woman, took a packet of blancmange powder, which he slipped into his pocket, and put the money down on the counter.

'Tell 'er when 'er comes,' he mumbled with his pipe still in his mouth, and out he shuffled. Timmy growled. The old man smelt very unwashed and Timmy didn't like him.

At last the sandwiches were finished and the old woman appeared again. She had packed them up neatly in four parcels of grease-proof paper, and had pencilled on each what they were. Julian read what she had written and winked at the others.

'My word – we're in for a grand time!' he said. 'Cheese, Pork, Ham and Egg – and what's this?'

'Oh, that's four slices of my home-made fruit cake,' said the old woman. 'I'm not charging you for that. It's just so that you can taste it!'

'It looks like half the cake!' said Julian, touched. 'But we shall pay for it, with many thanks. How much is all that?'

She told him. Julian put down the money and added five pence for the cake. 'There you are, and many thanks,' he said. 'And that money there was left by an old fellow with a clay pipe who took a packet of blancmange powder.'

'That would be Old Man Gupps,' said the woman. 'Well, I hope you'll enjoy your tour. Come back here if you want any more sandwiches cut! If you eat all those today you won't do badly!'

'Woof,' said Timmy, hoping that he too would share a few. The woman produced a bone for him, and he took it up in his mouth.

'Thanks!' Julian said. 'Come on – now we really start!'

Only one customer came in—a solemn old man smoking a clay pipe

Let's Make a Kite

KITES are always fun, especially if we make our own. They can be made in all sorts of shapes and sizes, but one of the best high-flyers is the simple diamond-shaped kite seen in the sketch. Here's how to make it.

You will need two thin bamboo canes – one about 2 ft. long, and the other 3 ft.

Tie the cross-bar cane very tightly to the upright cane, about 9 in. from the top. (See Fig. 1.)

Add the string outline as shown in Fig. 2. Be sure to keep the string as taut as possible.

For covering the framework you could use polythene or thin cotton material. (Perhaps Mum could find you an old summer dress!) Cut your material to shape, being sure to allow an extra inch or so all round for turning in over the string outline. Sew or stick down the overlap according to the kind of material you are using. Fig. 3 shows you how to cut the material.

Don't stretch the covering material too tightly over the framework. Allow a little play so that the material will billow out to catch the breeze in the same way as the sail of a boat.

Fig. 4 shows you where to fix the guide-line and tail; and Fig. 5 shows how to fold the paper tail-flights.

If your kite tends to 'nose-dive' instead of climb, just add two or three more flights to the tail.

Fig. 1

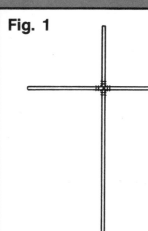

Fig. 2

STRING

Fig. 5

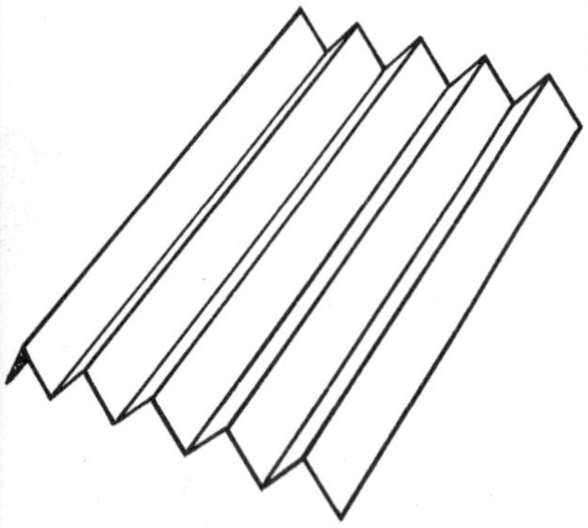

Fig. 4

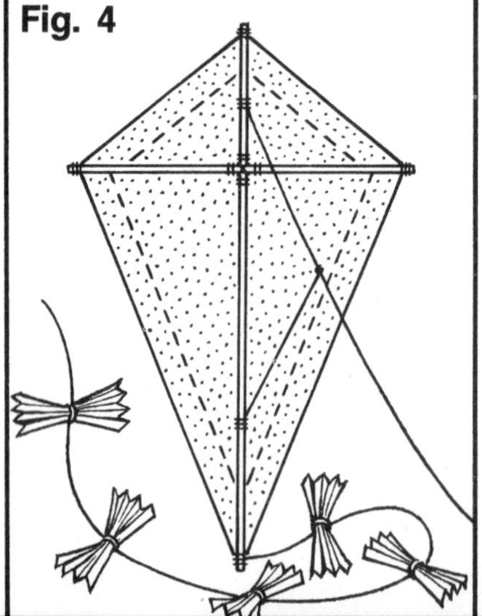

Fig. 3

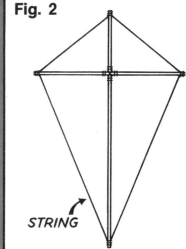

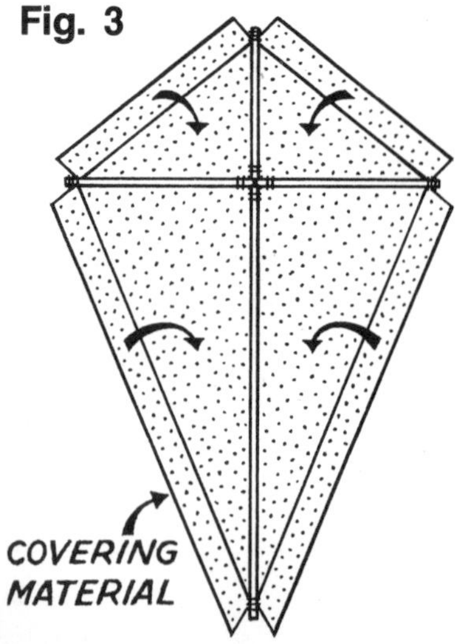

COVERING MATERIAL

Chapter 3
Across the Countryside

18

19

All About Foxes

ALTHOUGH a fox is a very wary creature, it is also extremely inquisitive. A strange sound, a new scent, or an object it hasn't seen before will arouse its curiosity immediately. When the Five spent the night in the cellar at Two-Trees it was not long before a wily old fox came nosing around to find out what was going on.

It is doubtful if there is any other wild animal in Britain that can outclass a fox in cunning or intelligence. If it was possible to train a fox as completely as one can a dog, it would make a truly remarkable pet. But a fox cannot be wholly tamed. Sooner or later the call of the wild will prove too strong. Within a few minutes of its escape, all its wild instincts will have returned and our pet will be a pet no longer.

Although many foxes are killed by hunts or destroyed by farmers and landowners, Reynard manages to hold his own. This is largely due to the animal's cunning and intelligence, and to the fact that the fox is mainly a creature of the night. Rocky coastlines are among their favourite haunts, for here they are safe from hounds and, to a large extent, from man.

A great many stories have been told of the cunning of the fox. There have been instances of foxes mastering the working of latches and gate fastenings. They have learnt to make spring traps harmless by rolling on them, or scratching earth and stones over them. A six-foot-high fence of wire netting around a poultry run can be child's play for a wily fox – it will scramble up the mesh as easily as humans can climb a ladder!

It is when the hounds are on its trail that a fox shows its greatest cunning. One trick is to run along the bed of a stream in order to destroy its scent. Yet another clever ruse is to submerge itself in a pond with only the tip of its nose above water.

One fox on the run from pursuing hounds was seen to run for a long distance along a length of rail metal in order to leave no tell-tale scent on the ground.

Did you know that a fox is a first-class mimic? It can imitate the cries of several creatures of the wild if it suits its purpose. It has been claimed that a fox can imitate the bleat of a young lamb so realistically that it can deceive even a shepherd.

If you live in the country it is likely that you will hear the call of a fox more often than you will see the animal itself. The dog-fox can be heard at night barking, with a sharp *yip-yip*, repeated two, three, or perhaps four times in succession. During the months of January and February, which is Reynard's courting time, the vixen utters a call which can best be described as a scream. It is a short, spine-chilling cry, usually repeated several times running.

Some readers may think that foxes are strictly flesh-eaters, with a preference for poultry and young lambs. But, like badgers, their diet is very mixed and they eat a fair amount of vegetable matter, including grass and wild fruits. Rats, mice, rabbits, moles, birds and their eggs, are all on a fox's menu. It has even found a way of unrolling a hedgehog.

Unlike the badger, a fox is not the slightest bit house-proud. It will allow its den to become cluttered with unsavoury remains of its meals – an evil-smelling collection of bones, feathers and fur. One way of telling which is a fox's or a badger's hole is by its unpleasant smell! The fox itself has a strong musky odour, too.

Watching foxes is not as easy as watching badgers. Brock lives at the same address the whole year round, but it is only between about March and July, when the cubs are being reared, that you can hope to find the fox family in the same place.

One of the reasons why farmers and poultry-keepers have a grudge against foxes is because they will often kill far more hens, ducks or geese than they need. They may kill half a dozen or more but only carry off one.

A fox may have a bad reputation, but it is a very beautiful and intelligent animal. As for the cubs – even anti-fox people fall for their charms!

The Story of Maps

Julian took jolly good care not to leave his map behind when the Five set out on their exciting weekend hike. It was Julian's map that showed them the whereabouts of that mysterious lake, Gloomy Water.

To an experienced map-reader, a map is far more than a means of finding one's way. When you get to know what all the various signs and symbols mean, the maze of printed detail is transformed into wooded valleys, heathland and meadow; you can see churches with towers and churches with steeples, historic old castles and windmills. Besides seeing your route, you can also get a very good idea of the scenery and places of interest on the way.

Think for a moment of the

A surveyor uses a theodolite to measure angles from an ordnance survey triangulation pillar

millions of people who have to rely on maps – surveyors, engineers, air pilots, the armed forces, oil prospectors, explorers, and long-distance lorry drivers, to name but a few. Without its charts, a ship would very soon be in trouble from rocks, shallows and tricky harbour approaches.

Map-making is as old as the earliest civilisations. In early Bible times, plans were scratched on clay tablets. For thousands of years before the birth of Christ, the Egyptian scribes prepared maps and route reports on pieces of wood or on a very crude form of paper called papyrus, and these maps were surprisingly accurate.

As far as is known, the first attempt at preparing a map of the world was made in the sixth century B.C. It is believed to have been the work of Alexander of Miletus. He made the Aegean Sea the centre of the world, bounded by the Caspian Sea to the east and the Tin Islands (thought to be the Scilly Isles) to the west.

The medieval map-makers really went to town. Nothing less than the whole of the then known earth satisfied them – they even included the Garden of Eden, and put Jerusalem as the centre of the earth. Regions for which they had no details were filled in with fantastic drawings of dragons and sea-serpents. Winds were represented by cherubs with puffed-out cheeks, or by ships with billowing sails.

As works of art they deserved full marks, but, alas, they were

of little practical use, for they were in no way reliable. For example, one showed Great Britain roughly in its correct position, but upside down, with London set right in the middle of the country where Birmingham stands today!

It was the outcome of the Rebellion in 1745 that really started serious map-making in England. When Pretender Charles Stuart landed in Scotland to claim the throne of his ancestors, the King of England sent an army of Redcoats north to arrest him. The rebels lured the Redcoats into wild, unmapped country, and the force was wiped out chiefly because they were unaware that an excellent way of retreat lay close at hand. One good map would have saved hundreds of lives.

The Government immediately ordered that the Highlands of Scotland should be mapped without delay to ensure that such a disaster should not happen again. Later, the mapping of the whole of England was ordered, and a special department, known as Ordnance Survey, was set up in 1791 to prepare maps of Britain in a uniform and accurate manner. Priority was given to the mapping of Kent and part of Sussex in case of a possible invasion of this area by the French.

This, the first English Ordnance map, was printed in 1800. It was not until seventy years later that maps of all parts of the country were completed. And it was not until 1892 that maps were printed in colours.

For many years past, Ord-

A rotary machine prints maps at speed

nance Survey have been engaged on the biggest job they have ever undertaken. This is the remapping of our rural areas to a scale of 25 inches to the mile, and urban areas to a scale of 50 inches to the mile. Another remapping task covers mountainous and moorland areas at a scale of 6 inches to the mile.

Some idea of the enormous amount of work involved will be gathered from the fact that it requires between 5,000 and 6,000 50-inch maps to cover the London area alone, about 40,000 sheets for our built-up areas, and over 200,000 for the rural areas.

The majority of maps we use for hiking and motoring are printed to a scale of one inch to the mile.

All our maps are built up from a system of triangles. The baseline from which surveys are made is situated on Salisbury Plain and has an exact length of six miles. From this line is built up a continuous network of triangles covering every part of the country. In 1870, the face of Britain was divided into 250 triangular areas, and since then

these have been further divided. The numerous concrete pillars (called trigonometrical points) we see up and down the country mark the corners of these smaller triangles.

One of the first jobs in mapmaking is done by teams of men who slowly work their way across the countryside taking measurements and noting down all the information which is to be included in the map. A field team may consist of twelve men, each responsible for

different parts of the survey. Drawings in the field are done on aluminium plates. These are taken back to the office where they are photographed by a giant camera.

From the photograph what is known as a 'fair copy' is prepared by a team of draughtsmen. After this has been very carefully checked it is photographed and used to make the actual printing plate.

If a map is to be printed in one colour only, one plate will be sufficient; but as many as ten colours may be used, so ten different plates may be needed – one for each colour. The actual printing must be done with absolute precision. Every one of the ten colours must be printed with 'spot-on' accuracy. There's no room for even the slightest error at any stage in map-making.

Your map will never let you down. It is a true and trusted friend, always at your service to make your wanderings through the countryside more interesting and exciting. That's what maps did for the Five, anyway!

A stereo plotting machine, on which a pen automatically draws the true position of a feature on a map

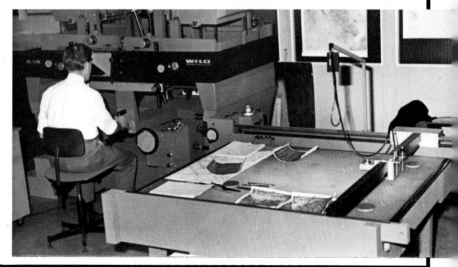

Interesting Inn Signs

THE Five are not likely to forget the *Three Shepherds* inn at the little village of Beacons, for it was there that they had a simply scrumptious breakfast of porridge and cream, eggs and bacon, and honey and home-baked bread.

Why the inn was called the *Three Shepherds* we do not know, but we can be pretty certain there is an interesting explanation. Actually, the meaning of lots of Britain's old inn signs leaves us guessing. Some, indeed, seem utterly ridiculous. Why, for example, are there signs such as *Elephant and Castle, Goat and Compasses* or *Pig and Whistle*? In almost every case you will find that even the most puzzling sign has an interesting story behind it – and sometimes a very surprising one, too!

Inn signs are a reminder of the days when most people could neither read nor write, so traders had to hang some kind of sign or symbol outside their premises to tell people the nature of their business. Perhaps you have seen the sign *The Crooked Billet*. A 'billet' is a log of wood and it was a log of wood that early ale-house keepers hung outside their premises. Owners of inns that sold beer displayed a bush or a bunch of green leaves.

This worked very well until two inns both selling the same type of drink opened up near each other. In this case one of the two landlords would try and think of a different kind of sign to that of his rival. Gradually inn signs became more varied and interesting as one landlord tried to outdo another with impressive signs.

But what about such teasers as *Elephant and Castle* or *Goat and Compasses*? The first-mentioned is the crest of the 500-year-old Ancient Company of Cutlers and the latter is a crest combining the arms of the Ancient Companies of Cordwainers (shoe-makers) and Carpenters. *Adam and Eve* is a sign very common in London. This is another 'Ancient Company' crest – that of the Fruiterers, which came into existence more than 450 years ago.

The very curious sign *Bag O' Nails* seems just nonsense. It isn't – it is, in fact, a very ancient sign. But in the beginning it wasn't *Bag O' Nails* – it was *Bachanals*, (referring to Bacchus, the god of wine). Over the years the pronunciation of the name Bachanals gradually changed (or became corrupted,

Eagle and Child

as we say) until it ended up as Bag O' Nails!

In parts of Derbyshire you will find a very baffling sign – *Eagle and Child*. It is a very ancient sign and the story is that in the fifteenth century a child was found in an eagle's nest on the estate of one of the Earls of Derby.

Another puzzling sign is *The Hole in the Wall*. It is believed to refer to the hole in the wall of old-time debtors' prisons, through which prisoners received gifts of food and other comforts from friends outside.

Collecting the names of Britain's inns makes a fascinating hobby, especially if you track down the meaning behind the sign. There are around 75,000 inns in Britain today and every one has a name and probably a pictorial sign as well, so it's a hobby that could last a lifetime!

The Crooked Billet

Chapter 4

George Is Worried

THEY lazed for some time in the sun after they had finished their meal. There were three sandwiches each left, and half a piece each of the fruit cake. No one had been able to manage a whole piece, much as they would have liked to.

Timmy seemed to think he could finish all the cake that was left, but Julian said no. 'It's such a gorgeous cake it would be really wasted on Timmy,' he said. 'You've had enough, Tim. Greedy dog!'

'Woof,' said Timmy, wagging his tail, and eyeing the cake watchfully. He sighed when he saw it being packed up. He had only had a bit of George's half-slice – what a cake!

'I'll pack three sandwiches and a half-slice of the cake into each of four bags,' said Julian. 'Anyone can eat his or hers whenever they like. I expect we shall have a good meal at the farm-house I've chosen for tonight, so you can eat when you like before then.'

'I don't feel as if I could eat anything till tomorrow morning,' said Anne, putting her bag of food into her rucksack. 'But it's odd how hungry you keep on getting, even if you feel you can't possibly be for hours and hours.'

'Well, Timmy can wolf anything you don't want,' said Julian. 'Nothing wasted when Tim's about. Now are we all ready? We're going through a little village soon, where we'll stop for a drink. I could do with a ginger-beer. And then on we go to our farm-house. We ought to

try and arrive about five, because it gets dark so soon.'

'What's the farm-house called!' asked Anne.

'Blue Pond Farm,' said Julian. 'Nice name, isn't it? I hope it's still got a blue pond.'

'Suppose they haven't room for us?' said Anne.

'Oh, they can always put a couple of girls somewhere,' said Julian. 'Dick and I can sleep in a barn if necessary. We're not particular!'

'*I'd* like to sleep in a barn too,' said Anne. 'I'd love to. Let's not ask for a bedroom, let's all sleep in a barn – on straw or hay or something.'

'No,' said Julian. 'You girls will have to be in the house. It gets cold at night, and we've brought no rugs. We boys will be all right with our macs over us. I'm not letting you two girls do that.'

'It's *stupid* being a girl!' said George, for about the millionth time in her life. 'Always having to be careful when boys can do as they like! I'm going to sleep in a barn, anyway. I don't care what you say, Ju!'

'Oh yes you do,' said Julian. 'You know quite well that if ever you go against the orders of the chief – that's me, my girl, in case you didn't know it – you won't come out with us again. You may look like a boy and behave like a boy, but you're a girl all the same. And like it or not, girls have got to be taken care of.'

'I should have thought that boys hated having to take care of girls,' said George, sulkily. 'Especially girls like me who

don't like it.'

'Well, decent boys like looking after their girl cousins or their sisters,' said Julian. 'And oddly enough decent girls like it. But I won't count you as a girl, George, decent or otherwise. I'll merely count you as a boy who's got to have an eye on him – my eye, see? So take that look off your face, and don't make yourself any more difficult than you already are.'

George couldn't help laughing, and the sulky look went at once. She gave Julian a punch.

Timmy seemed to think he could finish all the cake that was left, but Julian said 'no'

'All right. You win. You're so jolly domineering these days I feel quite afraid of you!'

'You're not afraid of anyone,' said Dick. 'You're the bravest girl I ever knew! Aha! That's made old George blush like a girl! Let me warm my hands, George!'

And Dick held his hands up in front of George's scarlet face, pretending to warm them at her fiery blush. She didn't know whether to be pleased or angry. She pushed his hands away and got up, looking more like a boy than ever with her short tousled hair and her well-freckled face!

The others got up and stretched. Then they settled their rucksacks on their backs again, with their macs fastened to them, threw their blazers over their shoulders and set off down Fallaway Hill.

Timmy followed, but he didn't bound about as usual. He went slowly and carefully. George looked round for him, and frowned.

'What *is* the matter with Timmy?' she said. 'Look at him! Not a jump or a scamper in him!'

They all stopped and watched him. He came towards them and they saw that he was limping slightly with his left hind leg. George dropped down beside him and felt the leg carefully.

'I think he must have twisted it – sprained it or something, when he was down that rabbit-hole,' she said. She patted him gently on the back and he winced.

'What's the matter, Tim?' said George, and she parted the hair on his back, examining the white skin underneath to see why he had winced when she had patted him.

'He's got an awful bruise here,' she said at last, and the others bent to see. 'Something must have hurt his back down in that hole. And Anne must have hurt one of his legs when she held on to them and dragged him out. I *told* you not to hold on to his legs, Anne.'

'Well, how were we to get him out if I didn't?' demanded Anne, feeling cross but rather guilty. 'Did you want him to stick there for days and days?'

'I don't think there's much damage done,' said Julian, feeling the hind leg. 'I honestly think he's only just twisted it a bit, George. He'll be all right after tonight, I'm sure.'

'But I must be *certain*,' said George. 'Did you say we come to a village soon, Ju?'

'Yes – Beacons Village,' said Julian. 'We can ask if there's a vet anywhere in the district if you like. He'll look at Timmy's leg and tell you if there's anything much wrong. But I don't think there is.'

'We'll go on to the village then,' said George. 'Oh dear – the only time I *ever* wish Timmy was a *little* dog is when he's hurt – because he's so very very heavy to carry.'

'Well, don't think of carrying him yet,' said Dick. 'He can walk on three legs even if he can't on

'He's got an awful bruise here,' she said at last, and the others bent to see

26

four! He's not as bad as all that, are you, Timmy?'

'Woof,' said Timmy, mournfully. He was rather enjoying all the fuss. George patted his head. 'Come on,' she said, 'we'll soon get that leg put right. Come on, Tim.'

They all went on, looking round to see how Timmy was getting on. He followed slowly, and then began to limp more badly. Finally he lifted his left hind leg up from the ground and ran on three legs only.

'Poor boy,' said George. 'Poor Timmy! I do hope his leg will be all right tomorrow. I can't possibly go on with the hike if it isn't.'

It was rather a gloomy company that came to Beacons Village. Julian made his way to a little inn that stood in the middle, called "Three Shepherds".

A woman was shaking a duster out of a window. Julian called up to her.

'I say! Is there a vet anywhere in this district! I want someone to have a look at our dog's leg.'

'No. No vet here,' answered the woman. 'Not one nearer than Marlins over six miles away.'

George's heart sank. Timmy would never be able to walk six miles.

'Is there a bus?' she called.

'No. Not to Marlins,' said the woman. 'No bus goes there, missy. But if you want your dog's leg seen to, you go up to Spiggy House, up along there. Mr. Gaston lives there with his horses, and he knows about dogs too. You take the dog there. He'll know what to do.'

'Oh *thank* you,' said George, gratefully. 'Is it very far?'

'About half a mile,' said the woman. 'See that hill? You go up there, take the turning to the right and you'll see a big house.

That's Spiggy House. You can't mistake it because of the stables built all round it. Ask for Mr. Gaston. He's nice, he is. Maybe you'll have to wait a little if he's out with his horses though – he may not be in till it's almost dark.'

The four held a little council. 'We'd better go up to this Mr. Gaston's, I think,' said Julian. 'But I think you and Anne, Dick, should go on to the farm-house I planned to stay in for the night, and make arrangements for us. We don't want to leave it till the last minute. I'll go with George and Timmy, of course.'

'Right,' said Dick. 'I'll take Anne now. It will be dark pretty soon. Got your torch, Julian?'

'Yes,' said Julian. 'And I'm pretty good at finding my way, as you know. I shall come back to this village after we've been to Mr. Gaston's, and then make straight for the farm-house. It's about a mile and a half away.'

'Thanks awfully for saying you'll come with me, Julian,' said George. 'Let's go now, shall we? Well, Dick and Anne – see you later!'

Julian set off with George and Timmy up the hill to Spiggy House. Timmy went on three legs, and still seemed very sorry for himself. Anne and Dick watched him, feeling sorry for him.

'I hope he's all right tomorrow,' said Dick. 'It will spoil our week-end if he's not, no doubt about that!'

They turned away and walked through the little village of Beacons. 'Now for Blue Pond Farm-house,' said Dick. 'Julian didn't give me very clear directions. I think I'll ask someone exactly where it is.'

But they met nobody except a man driving a little cart. Dick

'Are we on the right road for Blue Pond Farmhouse?' shouted Dick

hailed him and he pulled up his horse.

'Are we on the right road for Blue Pond Farm-house?' shouted Dick.

'Ar,' answered the man, nodding his head.

'Is it straight on – or do we take any paths or little lanes?' asked Dick.

'Ar,' said the man, nodding again.

'What does he mean – "ar"?' said Dick. He raised his voice again.

'Is it this way?' and he pointed.

'Ar,' said the man again. He raised his whip and pointed up the road where the two were going, and then across to the west.

'Oh, I see – we turn to the right up there?' called Dick.

'Ar,' said the man, nodding, and drove on so suddenly that the horse almost stepped on Dick's foot.

'Well – if we find the farm-house after all those "ars" we'll be clever,' said Dick. 'Come on!'

Training Your Dog

CHASING rabbits was one of Timmy's greatest joys, even though he never caught one. It was a thrill he couldn't resist. But one word of rebuke from George, or any other member of the Five, and he would give up the chase immediately. Timmy had been so well trained that he would obey *any* order they gave him.

A dog is said to be man's best friend. If well trained it will be just that. On the other hand, an *untrained* dog can lead its owner a dog's life! It will bark its head off at everyone who calls at the house, pester for scraps at meal-times, scramble over furniture, annoy neighbours and generally make itself a nuisance.

In nine cases out of ten it is the owner's fault, not the dog's. "He's only a puppy – he'll soon grow out of it," is a common excuse. Don't believe it – it is more likely to grow *into* it than out of it! The older a dog becomes, the more difficult it is to train it.

Before you start training a dog, you should know some important facts. First, no dog is 'almost human', as we say. It is not nearly as intelligent as proud owners often claim. It is not much good at reasoning things out for itself. At the same time, it can be *taught* to do lots of tricks by a person who understands how a dog's mind works.

"What a clever dog!" people say when they see it carrying a newspaper or a basket of groceries, for example. Actually, it is a case of a clever *owner,* not a clever dog!

Never use a stick to punish a dog. A slap with your hand or a newspaper is the limit. If possible, make use of stern, scolding words instead. No dog likes this. If punishment has to be given, give it immediately. If you delay, the dog will have no idea why it is being puished. Punishment must be given on the spot, at the time the dog misbehaves.

For example, if your dog has gone chasing after a chicken, it is not the slightest use calling it back and then punishing it. What happened a minute or so

A guide dog trainer gives an Alsatian a lesson in kerb drill

earlier is ancient history as far as the dog is concerned. The result is that it thinks it has had a wigging for coming back when called! That's how a dog's mind works. You simply must remember this before giving praise or a scolding.

When you are giving obedience training, use one-word commands, and always the *same* word. The four most important words of command are *Come, Stay, Sit* and *Down* (lie down). If you make the mistake of saying "Sit down", the dog won't know whether to sit down or lie down!

House training must begin the very day your puppy arrives. You must expect a few puddles at first, but if you persist in taking the dog outside before, or immediately after, the 'accident' occurs, it will soon get the right idea!

It is not much use starting obedience training before the age of four months, as a puppy is far too playful and scatter-brained up to that age. On the other hand, if you leave training too late, the dog may have formed habits of its own which

no amount of scolding will break.

Make a rule never to use tit-bits as a reward when carrying out obedience training. 'Cupboard-love' obedience is not what we want. A dog should obey because it wants to please you. Reward your dog with a friendly pat and plenty of praise.

Let's start with the order *Stay.* Make the dog lie down in front of you, with its lead slack in your hand. Raise a warning fore-finger and order "Stay!", then walk backwards as far as the lead will allow. If the dog stays put, praise it, then lay the lead on the ground and walk back a little further. You will have some failures, but in time you should be able to retreat right out of sight without the dog moving.

Now for the order *Down.* Put the dog on the lead. Hold the lead in the right hand, with the slack of the lead under the instep of your shoe. Give the order "Down" and pull on the lead with your right hand, at the same time pushing down on the dog's shoulders with your left hand. This will force the dog

into a lying position. Then pile on the praises and repeat the operation.

To teach the order *Sit,* pull back on the collar with one hand, at the same time pressing down on the dog's rump with your other hand. Then it's a matter of praise and repeat.

"Come!" is perhaps the most important comand of all. A dog that doesn't come when called is a nuisance to its owner and a danger to itself. Sit the dog in front of you, with a long length of cord added to its lead. Start by pulling gently on the lead and ordering "Come". Next time, stand farther back and pull on the cord. Praise or scold as necessary and continue to stand further away each time. Later on you should remove the lead, leaving the dog free, and move a considerable distance away, perhaps even out of sight. Right from the start, insist on instant obedience. A 'come-when-it-thinks-it-will' (or not-at-all!) dog is a constant source of trouble to its owner.

With patience, kindness and understanding, yours could become a dog like Timmy!

Pot~Shot Table Game

All you need is a cardboard box (a shoe box would be suitable), a few marbles and a wooden rod about a foot long. Cut the openings in the box and give them score numbers as shown. Use the cue as you would in billiards. A marble must go right inside the box to score. The winner could be the first to reach 100, or whoever makes top score with an agreed number of marbles.

Be Your Own Weather

Cirrus

As you can imagine, the weather was very important to the Five when they went hiking or looking for some new adventure. Fortunately, Julian could always be relied upon to foretell sunshine or shower. He had learnt how to interpret lots of the 'advance weather' messages that nature supplies.

You, too, could become your own weather prophet! Here are a few tips on keeping your 'weather-eye' open.

Whether we live in town or country we can very often obtain some reliable clues concerning the weather on the way. Even in the heart of a large city we can see the clouds – and clouds are very reliable weather indicators. Here are five different cloud formations, with notes on the weather they foretell.

Cirrus (often called 'Mare's Tails'). They are the highest clouds of all, and being over 25,000 feet above the earth are composed of ice crystals. Usually they appear in the sky as straight, or slightly curved, parallel streaks, and they are the first and last to pick up and reflect the rays of the rising and setting sun.

If they appear during a hot, dry spell, you can be sure a change is on the way, though there will probably be more wind than rain. They are, in fact, advance messengers of a storm centre, but the disturbance may be hundreds of miles behind them.

Cirro-Cumulus. This formation is commonly known as 'Mackerel Sky', as the cloudlets

Cirro-Cumulus

look like the scales of a fish. Their message? Warmer and more settled weather is on the way.

Stratus. These are long, horizontal white clouds, often seen in the late evening after a warm day. They are the lowest cloud-type of all, and are formed by the cooling of moist air over watery regions. Always a welcome sight, for tomorrow should be a lovely day!

Cumulus. These are the billowy-white clouds that drift across the sky on a summer's day. As long as they remain light and fluffy, the rest of the day should be fine. But if they lose their cotton-wool appearance, and become greyish with hard outlines, then rain can be expected.

Nimbus. Grey and gloomy; their message is gloomy, too! At the best, drizzle; at the worst, a downpour.

Fast-moving clouds usually foretell a rapid change in the weather, for better or worse, as the case may be.

The tints of the sky can also tell us something of weather on the way. If the dawn sky is flushed with delicate shades of pink and green, a wet and stormy day is probable. A pale pink dawn tells of wind rather than rain. A yellow tint in the sky at any time of day is a warning that raincoats will soon be needed.

If, at night, you see a circular 'rainbow' (known as a 'corona') around the moon, take note whether its diameter expands or contracts. If it expands, rain is to

Cumulus

be expected; if it contracts, brighter weather should have arrived by dawn.

Bees and spiders are good weather prophets. Bees seldom fly far from their hives if rain is coming. If, in the early morning, you see strands of spiders' web trailing over the grass and bushes, you will know that the spiders consider the weather

30

Prophet

favourable for venturing further afield than usual.

Chimney smoke rising straight up into the air is another promise of a fine day. Swallows catch insects in the air. When fine weather is sure, insects fly high – and the swallows have to fly high to catch them. When swallows swoop low over the ground, this is a sign that the insects sense that rain is to be expected.

If stars appear to 'twinkle' more than usual, it will probably be raining before dawn. In the daytime, especially towards late afternoon, you may notice that distant objects appear to stand out bold and clear, and seem to be much nearer than they actually are. Such conditions are a warning that rain is not far away – probably heavy, too.

Hang a few fir cones in your porch. Their 'petals' open when dry weather is at hand, but close tightly when rain is on the way. Seaweed is a good 'barometer', too. It feels crisp and dry during fine weather, but becomes limp and damp as wet weather approaches.

And, of course, it's sure to rain if we leave our macs at home!

Nimbus

A Cool Box for Campers

EVERY camper knows the difficulty of keeping perishable foods cool and fresh in hot weather. Butter becomes an oily mess, milk goes sour and bread becomes as dry as sawdust.

One answer is to make a cool-box as illustrated here. It is not claimed to be in the same class as your refrigerator at home, but it *will* keep food at a much lower temperature than the outside air.

All you need is a wooden box, some sacking or perhaps an old blanket, and a few strips of cloth. Drape the box with the sacking, place a bowl of water on top of the box, and from the bowl trail the strips of cloth down the sides of the box. The more strips you have, the cooler will be the temperature inside the box.

The strips of cloth (any absorbent material will do) soak up water from the bowl and very soon saturate the material draping the box. This has the effect of lowering the temperature inside the box. All you have to do is to top up the bowl of water occasionally.

It is advisable to keep the box clear of the ground to prevent it being raided by creatures of the wild! You could mount it on a post, or suspend it from the branch of a tree. It should be mentioned that the thicker the draping material, the more efficiently will the cooler operate.

31

Chapter 5

Anne and Dick

34

Fun With Figures

FIGURES *can* be fun! Here are a few brain-teasers to try out on your friends.

Can you take 45 from 45 and still have 45 left? It's quite simple if you do it this way:

```
9+8+7+6+5+4+3+2+1=45
1+2+3+4+5+6+7+8+9=45
8+6+4+1+9+7+5+3+2=45
```

Here's another 'impossible' sum. Can you divide 8,888 by two and get nothing as the answer? All you have to do is to draw a line through the middle of the 8's which will turn them into 0's.

Thought-Reading Maths!

Tell one of your friends that if he works out a sum in his head you will read his thoughts and tell him the correct answer. He won't believe you, so you must prove it!

Say to your friend: "Think of a number. Double it. Add 20 (or *any* even number, as it makes no difference). Divide the answer by 2. Now take away the number you first thought of and your answer is . . ." To his amazement you give him the correct answer to his sum!

Your secret is that the answer will always be *half* of the number you tell your friend to add. Here is an example:

Think of a number 12
Double it 24
Add 40 64
Divide by 2 32
Take away number first
  thought of (12) 20

You knew the answer would be 20 because it is *half* of the 40 you told your friend to add! It makes no difference what numbers your friends first think of.

Square It Up!

Can you place the numbers 1 to 16 in a square so that the figures will add up to 34 across, down, or from corner to corner? Here's how it's done:

```
 1   8  13  12
14  11   2   7
 4   5  16   9
15  10   3   6
```

Figure This Out!

It is surprising how many people you can catch out with this little trick. Without warning, suddenly hand someone a pencil and a piece of paper and ask him to write down in *figures*, as quickly as possible, TEN THOUSAND, TEN HUNDRED AND TEN.

Most of your victims will fall into the trap and write 10,1010 – which is *not* the correct answer. The *ten hundred* part makes up another thousand, so the correct way to write it is 11,010.

?

Be an Amazing Age-Guesser!

With the aid of the chart below you will be able to 'guess' the ages of any of your friends providing they are not more than 21 years old. All you have to do is to ask someone to show you in which columns of the chart their age appears. Then simply add together the *top* numbers of the columns he has indicated.

Here is an example. Suppose that Julian, of the Famous Five, is aged 15 years. You will see that 15 is printed in four of the five columns. The numbers at the top of these four columns are: 1, 2, 4 and 8 – which add up to 15! It works every time!

1	2	4	8	16
3	3	5	9	17
5	6	6	10	18
7	7	7	11	19
9	10	12	12	20
11	11	13	13	21
13	14	14	14	22
15	15	15	15	23
17	18	20	24	24
19	19	21	25	25
21	22	22	26	26

Chapter 6

In the Middle of the Night

I'TS not bad,' said Anne. 'There's a fairly clean mattress and a rug. I'll be all right. But what about if the others come, Dick! Will you look out for them? I almost think George will have to sleep in a barn with you and Julian if she comes. That old woman won't let anyone else in, I'm sure!'

'I'll look out for them and arrange something,' said Dick. 'You eat the rest of your sandwiches and your cake, and see if you can dry your wet feet and make yourself really comfortable. There's a shed or something out here. I shall be quite all right. Yell for me if you want me.'

Anne went back into the room. She felt wet and tired, hungry and thirsty. She ate all her food, and had a drink from the jug. Then she felt sleepy and lay down on the mattress, throwing the rug over her. She meant to listen for the others to come, but she was too tired. She fell fast asleep!

Dick was prowling about down below. He was careful because he didn't want to run into the old woman's son. He didn't like the sound of him somehow! He came to a small barn with piles of straw in one corner. He flashed his torch cautiously round.

'This will do for me,' he thought. 'I can be quite comfortable here in that straw. Poor Anne! I wish old George was with her. I'd better wait about

and watch for the other two, or I'll fall asleep and miss them, once I bed down in that straw! It's only about six o'clock too – but we've had a long day. I wonder how Timmy is? I wish he was here!'

Dick thought that probably George and Julian would come in through the same gate as he and Anne had used. He found a broken-down shed near the gate and sat down on a box there, waiting for them to come.

He ate his sandwiches while he waited. They were very comforting! He ate every one and then the cake. He yawned. He felt very sleepy indeed, and his feet were wet and tired.

No one arrived at all – not even the old woman's son. She could still be seen sewing under

the lamp. But after about two hours, when it was almost eight o'clock, and Dick was beginning to be very worried about George and Julian, the old woman got up and put away her work-basket.

She disappeared out of Dick's sight, and didn't come back. But the light was still there, shining out of the window. Left for her son, probably, thought Dick.

He tiptoed to the window. The rain had stopped now and the night was much clearer. The stars were out and a moon was coming up. Dick's spirits rose.

He peered in at the lighted room. Then he saw the old woman lying on a broken-down sofa in a corner. A blanket was pulled right up to her chin and she seemed to be asleep. Dick

A bit of paper fluttered in at the broken pane

went back to his shed, but now he felt there was no use in watching for George and Julian. They must have lost their way completely! Or else Mr. Gaston, or whatever his name was, must have had to do something to Timmy's leg, and Julian had decided to stay at the inn in Beacons Village for the night.

He yawned again. 'I'm too sleepy to watch any more,' he decided. 'I shall fall off this box with sleep if I don't go and lie down in that straw. Anyway I think I'd hear if the others came.'

Using his torch cautiously again, he made his way to the barn. He shut the door behind

him and bolted it roughly from the inside by running a stick through two hasps. He didn't know why he did that – perhaps because he was still thinking of the old woman's bad-tempered son!

He flung himself down on the straw, and immediately fell asleep. Outside the sky became clearer and clearer. The moon came up, not fully, but large enough to give some light. It shone down on the desolate little stone house and ill-kept out-buildings.

Dick slept soundly. He lay in the soft straw and dreamed of Timmy and George and Blue Ponds and bells. Especially bells.

He awoke suddenly, and lay for a moment wondering where he was. What was this prickly stuff round him? Then he remembered – of course, it was straw and he was in a barn! He was about to cuddle down again when he heard a noise.

It was only a small noise – a scratching on the wooden walls of the barn perhaps. Dick sat up. Were there rats there? He hoped not!

He listened. The scratching seemed to come from *outside* the barn, not inside. Then it stopped. After an interval it began again. Then there came a gentle tapping at the broken window just above Dick's head.

He felt very startled. Rats scratched and scrabbled about – but they didn't tap on windows. Who was tapping so very very cautiously on the little window? He held his breath and listened, straining his ears.

And then he heard a voice – a hoarse whisper.

'Dick! Dick!'

Dick was amazed. Could it be Julian? If so, how in the world

did he know that he, Dick, was in the barn? He sat listening, stiff with surprise.

The tapping came again, and then the voice, a little louder. 'Dick! I know you're there. I saw you go in. Come here to the window – quiet, now!'

Dick didn't know the voice. It wasn't Julian's, and it certainly wasn't either George's or Anne's. Then how did the owner know *his* name and that he was there? It was astounding. Dick didn't know what to do!

'Buck up!' said the voice. 'I've got to go in half a tick. I've got that message for you.'

Dick decided to go nearer to the window. He was quite certain that he didn't want whoever it was outside to come into the barn. He cautiously knelt up in the straw and spoke just underneath the window.

'I'm here,' he said, trying to make his voice deep and grown-up.

'You've been long enough coming,' grumbled the one outside, and then Dick saw him through the window – just a face, dim and wild-eyed, with a round bullet-like head. He crouched back, thankful that the face couldn't see him in the darkness of the barn.

'Here's the message from Nailer,' said the voice. 'Two-Trees. Gloomy Water. Saucy Jane. And he says Maggie knows. He sent you this. Maggie's got one too.'

A bit of paper fluttered in at the broken pane. Dick picked it up in a daze. What *was* all this? Was he dreaming?

The voice came again, insistent and urgent. 'You heard all that, Dick? Two-Trees. Gloomy Water. Saucy Jane. And Maggie knows too. Now I'm going.'

There came the sound of someone cautiously creeping round the barn – and then there was silence. Dick sat amazed and bewildered. Who was this wild-eyed fellow, who called him by his name in the middle of the night and gave him extraordinary messages that meant nothing at all to a sleepy boy? But Dick was wide awake now. He stood up and looked out of the window. There was nothing and no one to be seen except the lonely house and the sky.

Dick sat down again and thought. He put his torch on cautiously and looked at the piece of paper he had picked up. It was a dirty half sheet, with pencil marks on it that meant nothing to Dick at all. Words were printed here and there, but they were all nonsense to him. He simply couldn't make head or tail of his visitor, his message or the bit of paper!

'I'm sure I must be dreaming,' thought Dick, and put the paper into his pocket. He lay back in his straw, cuddling in deep, because he had got cold by the window. He lay and thought for a while, puzzling over the curious happenings, and then he felt his eyes closing.

But before he was quite asleep, he heard cautious foot-steps again! Was that fellow back once more? This time some-one tried the door – but the wooden stick was in the hasps. Whoever it was outside shook the door and the stick fell out at once. The man shook the door again as if thinking it had stuck, and then opened it. He came inside and shut the door behind him.

Dick caught a quick glimpse of him. No – this wasn't the same man as before. This was a man with a head of thick hair. Dick hoped and prayed that he wouldn't come over to the straw.

He didn't. He sat down on a sack and waited. He talked to himself after a while, but Dick could only make out a word or two.

'What's happened?' he heard. 'How much longer do I wait?' Then there was a mumble and Dick could not catch a word.

'Wait, wait – that's all I do,' muttered the man, and he stood up and stretched himself. Then he went to the door and looked out. He came back and sat down on the sack again.

He sat still and quiet then, and Dick found his eyes closing once more. Was this part of a dream too? He didn't have time to think it out because he was suddenly in a real dream, walking along ringing bells and seeing trees in twos everywhere round him!

He slept heavily all night long. When morning came he awoke suddenly and sat up. He was alone in the barn. Where had the second visitor gone? Or *could* it all have been a dream?

He came inside and shut the door behind him

Chapter 7
In the Morning

Chapter 8
All Together Again

IT was wonderful to be all together again. Julian took hold of Anne's arm and squeezed it. 'All right, Anne?' he said, rather worried at her pale face.

Anne nodded. She felt better at once, now she had Julian, George and Timmy, as well as Dick. 'I'm only just terribly hungry,' she said.

'I'll ask for breakfast straight away,' said Julian. 'All news later!'

The woman who had leaned out of the window shaking a duster the evening before, came up to them. 'I expect it's a bit late for you,' said Julian. 'But we haven't had any breakfast. What have you got?'

'Porridge and cream,' said the woman. 'And our own cured bacon and our own eggs. Our own honey and the bread I bake myself. Will that do? And coffee with cream?'

'I could hug you,' said Julian, beaming at her. The others felt the same. They went into a small, cosy dining-room and sat down to wait. Soon a smell of frying bacon and hot strong coffee would come into the room — what joy!

'Your news first,' said Dick, patting Timmy. 'Did you get to Spiggy House? Was Mr. Gaston there?'

'No, he wasn't,' said Julian. 'He was out somewhere. He had a very nice wife who made us wait for him, and said he wouldn't mind in the least looking at Timmy when he came back. So we waited and waited.'

'We waited till half past seven!' said George, 'and we felt rather awkward because we thought it might be getting near their meal-time. And then at last Mr. Gaston came.'

'He was awfully kind,' said Julian. 'He looked at Timmy's leg, and then he did something, I don't know what — put it back into place, I suppose — and Timmy gave a yell and George flung herself on him, and Mr. Gaston roared with laughter at George . . .'

'Well, he was very *rough* with Timmy's leg,' said George. 'But he knew what he was doing, of course, and now Timmy is perfectly all right, except for that bruise on his back, and even that is getting better. He can run as well as ever.'

'I'm glad,' said Anne. 'I kept thinking of poor old Tim all last night.' She patted him, and he licked her lavishly and wetly.

'What did you do then?' asked Dick.

'Well, Mrs. Gaston insisted on us staying to supper,' said Julian. 'She simply wouldn't take no for an answer, and I must say that by that time we were jolly hungry. So we stayed — and we had a jolly good meal too. So did Timmy! You should have seen his tummy afterwards — as round as a barrel. Good thing it's gone down today or I was thinking of changing his name to Tummy.' They all laughed, George especially.

'Idiot,' she said. 'Well, we didn't leave till about nine o'clock. We didn't worry about you because we felt sure you would be safely at Blue Pond Farm-house and would guess we'd have to wait about with

Timmy. And when we got there and found you hadn't arrived – well, we *were* in a state!'

'And then we thought you must have found somewhere else for the night,' said Julian, 'but we thought if we heard nothing we'd go down to the police first thing this morning and report your disappearance!'

'So down we came – without any breakfast either!' said George. 'That shows how worried we were! Blue Pond Farm-house was nice. They gave us a bed each in two tiny little rooms, and Timmy slept with me, of course.'

A wonderful smell came creeping into the little dining-room, followed by the inn-woman carrying a large tray. On it was a steaming tureen of porridge, a bowl of golden syrup, a jug of very thick cream, and a dish of bacon and eggs, all piled high on crisp brown toast. Little mushrooms were on the same dish.

'It's like magic!' said Anne, staring. 'Just the very things I longed for!'

'Toast, marmalade and butter to come, and the coffee and hot milk,' said the woman, busily setting everything out. 'And if you want any more bacon and eggs, just ring the bell.'

'Too good to be true!' said Dick, looking at the table. 'For goodness' sake, help yourselves quickly, girls, or I shall forget my manners and grab.'

It was a wonderful breakfast – extra wonderful because they were all so ravenously hungry. There wasn't a word said as they spooned up their porridge and cream, sweetened with golden syrup. Timmy had a dishful too – he loved porridge, though he didn't like the syrup – it made his whiskers sticky!

'I feel better,' said Anne, looking at the porridge dish. 'The thing is – shall I have some more porridge and risk not enjoying my bacon and eggs so much – or shall I go straight on with bacon and eggs?'

'A difficult question,' said Dick. 'And one that I am faced with too. On the whole I think I'll go on with bacon and eggs – we can always have more of those if we want to – and those little mushrooms really do make my mouth water! Aren't we greedy? But how can anyone help that when they're so hungry?'

'You haven't told us a single word of what happened to *you* last night,' said Julian, serving out the bacon and eggs with a generous hand. 'Now that you've got something inside you, perhaps you feel able to tell us exactly why you ignored my instructions and didn't arrive where you were supposed to last night.'

'It's like magic!' said Anne

'You sound like our headmaster at school!' said Dick. 'The plain fact is – we got lost! And when we did finally arrive somewhere, we thought it was Blue Pond Farm-house, and we stayed the night there.'

'I see,' said Julian. 'But didn't the people there tell you it wasn't the right place? Just so that you could have let us know? You must have known that we would worry about you.'

'Well, the old woman there was stone-deaf,' explained Anne, attacking her bacon and eggs vigorously. 'She didn't understand a word we said, and as we thought it *was* Blue Pond Farm-house, we stayed there – though it was a horrible place. And *we* were worried because *you* didn't arrive!'

'A chapter of accidents,' said Julian. 'All's well that ends well, however.'

'Don't sound so pompous!' said Dick. 'Actually we had a pretty poor time, Ju. Poor Anne had to sleep in a little loft, and I slept in straw in a barn – not that I minded that – but – well, peculiar things happened in the night. At least – I *think* they did. I'm not really sure it wasn't all a dream.'

'What peculiar things?' asked Julian at once.

'Well – I think perhaps I'll tell you when we're on our way again,' said Dick. 'Now I think about it in full daylight I feel that either it was all a silly dream – or – well, as I said – something very peculiar.'

'You never told me, Dick!' said Anne, in surprise.

'Well, to tell you the truth I forgot about it because other things happened,' said Dick. 'Having to get away from that man, for instance – and wondering about Julian and

A stream ran down the middle of the valley

George – and feeling so hungry.'

'You don't sound as if you had a good night at all,' said George. 'It must have been awful, too, trying to find your way in the dark. It poured with rain, didn't it?'

'Yes,' said Anne, 'but oh – the thing that frightened me more than anything was the bells! Did you hear them Julian? They suddenly clanged out, and they made me terribly scared. I couldn't think what they were! Whatever were they ringing out for? They were so loud.'

'Didn't you know what they were ringing for?' said Julian. 'They were bells rung from the prison that nice old woman told us about – they were rung to tell everyone on the countryside that a prisoner had escaped! Lock your doors. Guard your folk.'

Anne stared at Julian in silence. So that was why the bells had made such a clamour and clangour. She shivered.

'I'm glad I didn't know that,' she said. 'I would have slept in the straw with Dick if I'd known there was an escaped prisoner. Have they caught him?'

'I don't know,' said Julian. 'We'll ask the inn-woman when she comes.'

They asked her, and she shook her head. 'No. He's not caught yet. But he will be. All the roads from the moor are guarded and everyone is on the watch. He was a robber who broke into houses and attacked anyone who tried to prevent him. A dangerous fellow.'

'Julian – is it all right to go hiking on the moors if there's an escaped prisoner about?' said Anne. 'I shan't feel very comfortable.'

'We've got Timmy,' said Julian. 'He would be strong enough to protect us from three prisoners if necessary! You needn't worry.'

'Woof,' agreed Timmy, at once, and thumped his tail on the floor.

At last everyone had finished breakfast. Even starving Anne couldn't manage the last bit of toast. She sighed happily. 'I feel myself again,' she announced. 'I can't say I feel very much like walking – but I know it would be good for me after that enormous meal.'

'Good or not, we're going on our way,' said Julian, getting up. 'I'll buy some sandwiches first.'

The inn-woman was delighted with their hearty praises. She gave them some packets of sandwiches and waved good-bye. 'You come again whenever you can,' she said. 'I'll always have something nice for you.'

The four went down the street and took a lane at the bottom. It wound about for a short way and then came into a valley. A stream ran down the middle of the valley. The children could hear it gurgling from where they stood.

'Lovely!' said Anne. 'Are you going along by the stream? I'd like to.'

Julian looked at his map. 'Yes – we could,' he said. 'I've marked the path to follow, and the stream joins it some way on. So if you like we could go along by it, though it will be very rough walking.'

They made their way to the stream. 'Now Dick,' said Julian, when they had left the path. 'What about telling us all those peculiar things that happened in the night? There's nobody about to hear – not a soul in sight. Let's hear everything. We'll soon tell you whether it was a dream or not.'

'Right,' said Dick. 'Well, here's the tale. It does sound pretty queer.

Listen . . .'

Chapter 9

Dick Surprises the Others

DICK began his tale – but it really was very difficult to hear it because they couldn't walk four abreast, as there was no path to follow.

In the end Julian stopped and pointed to a thick clump of heather. 'Let's go and sit there and hear Dick's story properly. I keep missing bits. No one can hear us if we sit here.'

They sat down and Dick started again. He told about the old woman who was afraid her son would be angry if she let them stay the night. He told about his bed in the straw.

'And now here comes the bit I think must have been a dream' he said. 'I woke up to hear a scratching noise on the wooden walls of the barn . . .'

'Rats or mice?' said George, and Timmy leapt up at once, of course. He was sure she had said the words to him!

'I thought that too,' said Dick. 'But then I heard a gentle tap-tap-tapping on the window.'

'How horrid,' said Anne. 'I shouldn't have liked that at all.'

'Neither did I,' said Dick. 'But the *next* thing I heard was my name being called! "Dick! Dick!" Just like that.'

'It *must* have been a dream then,' said Anne. 'There was no one there who knew your name.'

Dick went on. 'Well, then the voice said – "Dick! I know you're there. I saw you go in!" And it told me to go to the window.'

'Go on,' said Julian. He was puzzled. No one in the world but Anne could have known that Dick was in the barn – and it certainly wasn't Anne out there in the night!

'Well, I went to the window,' said Dick, 'and I saw, rather dimly, of course, a wild-eyed looking fellow. He couldn't see me in the darkness of the barn. I just mumbled, "I'm here," hoping he would think I was whoever he wanted.'

'What did he say next?' asked George.

'He said something that sounded stuff and nonsense,' said Dick. 'He said it twice. It was "Two-Trees. Gloomy Water. Saucy Jane." And he said "Maggie knows." Just like that!'

There was a silence. Then George laughed. 'Two-Trees! Gloomy Water! Saucy Jane – and Maggie knows about it! Well, it *must* have been a dream, Dick! You know it must. What do you think, Julian?'

'Well – it does sound a bit non-sensical to have someone come in the middle of the night and call Dick by name and give him a strange message that doesn't mean a thing to him!' said Julian. 'It sounds more dream-like than real. I'd say it was a dream too.'

Dick began to think they were right, and then a sudden thought struck him. He sat up straight. 'Wait a bit!' he said. 'I've remembered something! The man slipped a bit of paper through the broken pane of the window, and I picked it up!'

'Ah – that's different,' said Julian. 'Now – if you can't find that paper, it's all a dream and you dreamt the paper too – but if you *can* find it, well the whole thing is true. Very peculiar indeed – but true.'

Dick searched quickly in his pockets. He felt paper in one of them, and drew it out. It was a dirty, crumpled piece, with a few words on it and a few lines. He held it out to the others in silence, his eyes shining.

'Is this the paper?' asked Julian. 'My word – so you didn't dream it after all, then!'

He took the paper. Four heads bent over it to examine it. No, five – because Timmy wanted to see what they were all so interested in. He thrust his hairy head between Julian's and Dick's.

'I can't make any sense of this paper,' said Julian. 'It's a plan of some kind, I think – but what of, or where, it's impossible to know.'

'The fellow said that Maggie had one of these bits of paper too,' said Dick, remembering.

'Who in the wide world *is* Maggie?' said George, 'And why should Maggie know?'

'Any more to tell?' asked Julian, intensely interested now.

'Well – the son of the deaf old woman came into the barn later on,' said Dick. 'And he sat and waited and waited, and muttered and muttered – and then when I woke up he wasn't there. So I thought I must have dreamt him too. He didn't see me, of course.'

Julian pursed up his lips and frowned. Then Anne spoke excitedly.

'Dick! Ju! I think I know why the second man came into the barn. It was the *second* man that the wild-eyed man wanted to give the message to, and the bit of paper – not to Dick. He didn't want *Dick*. But he had seen him creep into the barn, and I suppose he thought Dick was the man he really wanted and that he was in the barn waiting for him!'

'That's all very well – but how did he know my name?' asked Dick.

'He didn't know it! He didn't know it was you at all!' said Anne, excitedly. 'The other man's name must have been Dick too! Don't you *see*? They must have planned to meet there, the wild-eyed man and

the old woman's son – and the first man saw Dick go in, so he waited a bit and then went and tapped on the window! And when he called "Dick! Dick!" of course Dick thought it was he that he wanted, and he took the message and everything! And then the other man, the real Dick came along – and was too late to meet the first one. *Our* Dick had met him and got the message!'

Anne was quite breathless after this long speech. She sat and stared at the others eagerly. Didn't they think she was right?

They did, of course. Julian clapped her on the back. 'Well worked out, Anne! Of course that's what happened.'

Dick suddenly remembered the boy they had met on the way down from the old woman's cottage to Beacons Village – the whistling boy. What had he said about the old woman and her son?

'Anne – what did that whistling boy say? Wait a bit – he said that was Mrs. Taggart's place – and he said we'd better not go there or her son would drive us off. And he said – yes, I remember now – he said "Dirty Dick we call him – he's a terror!" Dirty *Dick*? His name *must* be Dick then! Why didn't I think of it before?'

'That proves that Anne is right,' said Julian, pleased. Anne looked pleased too. It wasn't often that she thought of something clever before the others did!

They all sat thinking. 'Would this have anything to do with the escaped prisoner?' said George at last.

'It might,' said Julian. 'He might have been the prisoner himself, that fellow who came with the message. Did he say

who the message was from?'

'Yes,' said Dick, trying to remember. 'He said it was from Nailer. I think that was the name – but it was all given in whispers, you know.'

'A message from Nailer,' said Julian. 'Well – perhaps Nailer is in prison – a friend of the man who escaped. And maybe when he knew this fellow was going to make a dash for it, he gave him a message for someone – the man at that old cottage, son of the old woman. They may have had a prearranged plan.'

'How do you mean?' asked Dick, looking puzzled.

'Well – the old woman's son, Dirty Dick, may have known that when the bells rang out, this fellow was making a run for it – and would come to bring him a message. He was to wait in the barn at night if the bells rang, just in case it was Nailer's friend who had escaped.'

'Yes, I see,' said Dick. 'I think you're right. Yes, I'm sure you are. My word, I'm glad I didn't know that fellow at the window was an escaped convict!'

'And *you've* got the message from Nailer!' said Anne. 'What a peculiar thing! Just because we lost our way and went to the wrong place, you get a message from a prisoner given you by one who's escaped! It's a pity we don't know what the message means – or the paper either.'

'Had we better tell the police?' said George. 'I mean – it may be important. It might help them to catch that man.'

'Yes,' said Julian. 'I think we *should* tell the police. Let's have a look at our map. Where's the next village?'

He looked at the map for a minute. 'I think really we might as well go on with what I had planned,' he said. 'I planned we should reach this village here – Reebles, look – in time for lunch, in case we hadn't got sandwiches. We'd have gone there for drinks anyway. So I vote we just carry on with our ramble, and call in at Reebles police-station – if there is one – and tell them our bit of news.'

Timmy wanted to go after them, but George held his collar tightly

What do you say?'

They all got up. Timmy was glad. He didn't approve of this long sit-down so soon after breakfast. He bounded ahead in delight.

'His leg's *quite* all right,' said Anne, pleased. 'Well I hope it teaches him not to go down rabbit holes again!'

It didn't, of course. He had his head down half a dozen within the next half-hour, but fortunately he could get no farther,

and he was able to pull himself out quite easily.

The four saw little wild ponies that day. They came trotting over a hillock together, small and brown, with long manes and tails, looking very busy indeed. The children stopped in delight. The ponies saw them, tossed their pretty heads, turned one way all together and galloped off like the wind.

Timmy wanted to go after them, but George held his collar tightly. No one must chase those dear little wild ponies!

'Lovely!' said Anne. 'Lovely to meet them as suddenly as that. I hope we meet some more.'

The morning was as warm and sunny as the day before. Once again the four of them had to take off their blazers, and Timmy's tongue hung out, wet and dripping. The heather and wiry grass was soft underfoot. They followed the stream closely, liking its brown colour and its soft gurgling voice.

They bathed their hot feet in it as they ate one of their sandwiches at half past eleven. 'This is bliss!' said George, lying back on a tuft of heather with her feet lapped by the water. 'The stream is tickling my feet, and the sun is warming my face – lovely! Oh, get away, Timmy, you idiot! Breathing down my neck like that, and making my face so wet!'

The stream at last joined the path that led to the village of Reebles. They walked along it, beginning to think of dinner. It would be fun to have it in a little inn or perhaps a farm-house, and keep their sandwiches for tea-time.

'But first we must find the police-station,' said Julian. 'We'll get our tale told, and then we'll be ready for our meal!'

Chapter 10

An Angry Policeman

and a Fine Lunch

49

MINUTES LATER A MEAL WAS SECURED...

MA, THESE KIDS WANT TO KNOW IF YOU CAN GIVE 'EM A MEAL.

THEY LOOK DECENT ENOUGH— YES, SEND THEM IN. KEEP HOLD OF THE DOG, THOUGH.

FRIENDS, TIMMY, FRIENDS. DINNER HERE— PERHAPS A NICE BONE FOR YOU.

NOW I'VE NOT HAD TIME FOR COOKING TODAY, SO YOU'LL HAVE TO TAKE WHAT WE'VE GOT— A SLICE OF HOME-MADE MEAT PIE, HAM AND TONGUE, OR EGGS AND SALAD... THEN YOU COULD HAVE SOME OF MY BOTTLED RASPBERRIES AND CREAM, AND PERHAPS FRESHLY MADE CREAM CHEESE AND CRACKERS TO FINISH OFF. HOW'S THAT?

FANTASTIC! DON'T TELL US ANY MORE— YOU'RE SENDING MY TASTE-BUDS WILD!

LATER ON, AS THEY TUCKED INTO THE CHEESE AND BISCUITS, THE GIRL WHO HAD DIRECTED THEM TO THE FARM APPEARED— AND JULIAN HAD AN IDEA...

MY NAME'S MEG. I LIVE HERE WITH MY GRAN. ARE YOU ON HOLIDAY?

SORT OF. WE'RE WALKING OVER YOUR MOOR. WE'VE BEEN TO LOTS OF NICE PLACES— BUT THERE'S ONE WE HAVEN'T BEEN TO YET. DO YOU KNOW IT? IT'S CALLED 'TWO-TREES'.

WHAT'S THAT? 'TWO-TREES'? OH, THAT WAS A LOVELY PLACE ONCE, BUT IT'S ALL IN RUINS NOW. IT WAS BUILT BESIDE A LAKE IN THE MIDDLE OF THE MOORS— ALL DARK AND SPOOKY IT WAS... NOW WHAT WAS IT CALLED?

DICK TOOK A CALCULATED GUESS...

GLOOMY WATER?

THAT'S IT, GLOOMY WATER. ARE YOU THINKING OF GOING BY THERE? YOU BE CAREFUL, THEN— THERE'S MARSHLAND AROUND THERE, JUST WHEN YOU LEAST EXPECT IT. NOW WOULD YOU LIKE ANYTHING MORE TO EAT?

NO, THANK YOU, THAT WAS MARVELLOUS— THE BEST LUNCH WE'VE EVER HAD! NOW WE MUST SETTLE UP AND BE OFF.

OFF TO 'TWO-TREES' AND GLOOMY WATER, I HOPE. THAT WOULD BE REALLY EXCITING!

Chapter 11

Julian's Idea

ONCE outside the farm-house Julian looked round at the others. 'We'll find out how far Two-Trees is and see if we've got time to pay it a visit,' he said. 'If we have, we'll go along there and snoop round. If we haven't we'll go tomorrow.'

'How can we find out how far it is?' said Dick eagerly. 'Will it be on your map?'

'It may be marked there if the lake is big enough,' said Julian. They walked down the hill, and took a path that led once more over the moors. As soon as they were out of sight and hearing of anyone Julian stopped and took out his big map. He unfolded it and the four of them crouched over it as he spread it out on the heather.

'That nice old lady said it was in the middle of the moors,' said Julian. 'Also we know there's a lake or at any rate a big pool of some kind.'

His finger traced its way here and there on the map. Then George gave a cry and dabbed her finger down.

'There, look! It's not really in the middle. See – Gloomy Water! That must be it. Is Two–Trees marked as well?'

'No,' said Julian. 'But perhaps it wouldn't be if it's in ruins. Ruins aren't marked on maps unless they are important in some way. This can't be important. Well – that's certainly Gloomy Water marked there. What do you say? Shall we have a shot at going there this afternoon? I wonder exactly how far it is.'

'We could ask at the post-office,' said George. 'Probably once upon a time the postman had to take letters there. They might know. They could tell us the way to go.'

They went back to the village and found the post-office. It was part of the village store. The old man who kept it looked over the top of his glasses at the children.

'Gloomy Water! Now what be you wanting that for? A real miserable place it is, for all it was so fine years ago.'

'What happened to it?' asked Dick.

'It was burnt,' said the old man. 'The owner was away, and only a couple of servants were there. It flared up one night, no one knows how or why – and was burnt almost to a shell. Couldn't get a fire-engine out there, you see. There was only a cart-track to the place.'

'And wasn't it ever built up again?' asked Julian. The old man shook his head.

'No. It wasn't worth it. The owner just let it fall to rack and ruin. The jackdaws and the owls nest there now, and the wild animals snuggle in the ruins. It's a queer place. I once went out to see it, hearing tales of lights being seen there. But there was nothing to see but the shell of the place, and the dark blue water. Ah, Gloomy Water's a good name for that lake!'

'Could you tell us the way? And how long would it take us to get there?' asked Julian.

'What for do you want to go and gaze at a poor old ruin?' said the old man. 'Or do you want to bathe in the lake? Well, don't you do so – it's freezing cold!'

'We just thought we'd go and see Gloomy Water,' said Julian. 'Such a strange name. Which is the way, did you say?'

'I didn't say,' said the old fellow. 'But I will if so be you're set on it. Where's your map? Is that one in your hand?'

Julian spread it out. The old fellow took a pen from his waistcoat pocket and began to trace a path over the moor. He put crosses here and there.

'See them crosses? They mark marshland. Don't go treading there, or you'll be up to your knees in muddy water! You follow these paths I've inked in for you and you'll be all right. Keep your eyes open for deer – there's plenty about those parts, and pretty things they are too.'

'Thank you very much,' said Julian, folding up the map. 'How long would it take us to get there from here?'

'Matter of two hours or more,' said the old man. 'Don't you try to go this afternoon. You'll find yourselves in darkness coming back, and with them dangerous marshy bits you're in danger all the time!'

'Right,' said Julian. 'Thanks very much. Er – we're thinking of doing a bit of camping, as the weather is so beautiful. I suppose you couldn't hire us a groundsheet or two and a few rugs?'

The other three stared at him in astonishment. Camping out? Where? Why? What was Julian thinking of all of a sudden?

Julian winked at them. The old man was ferreting about in a cupboard. He pulled out two large rubber ground-sheets and four old rugs. 'Thought I had them somewhere!' he said. 'Well, better you camping out in

52

October than me! Be careful you don't catch your deaths of cold!'

'Oh thanks – just what we want,' said Julian, pleased. 'Roll them up, you others. I'll settle up for them.'

Dick, Anne and George folded up the ground-sheets and the rugs in astonishment. Surely – surely Julian wasn't thinking of camping out by Gloomy Water? He must think the message that Dick had been given was very important!

'Julian!' said Dick, as soon as they got outside. 'What's up? What's all this for?'

Julian looked a little sheepish. 'Well – something suddenly came over me in the store,' he said. 'I suddenly felt we ought to go to Gloomy Water and snoop round. I felt excited somehow. And as we've got so little time this week-end I thought if we took things and camped out in the ruin we might make more of our few days.'

'What an idea!' said George. 'Not go on with our hiking, do you mean?'

'Well,' said Julian. 'If we find nothing, we *can* go on with our hike, of course. But if there's anything interesting, it's up to us to unearth it. I'm quite sure there's something up at Two-Trees.'

'We might meet Maggie there!' said Anne, with a giggle.

'We might!' said Julian. 'I feel quite free to go and investigate on our own seeing that we've made our report to the police, and it's been turned down with scorn. *Somebody* ought to follow up that message – besides Maggie!'

'Dear Maggie,' said Dick. 'I wonder who in the wide world she is!'

'Somebody worth watching if she's the friend of convicts,' said

Julian, more soberly. 'Look, this is what I thought we'd do – buy some extra food, and go along to Gloomy Water this afternoon, arriving there before dark. We'll find a good place to shelter in – there must be some good spot in the old ruin – and get heather or bracken for beds. Then tomorrow we can be up bright and early to have a look round.'

'It sounds smashing,' said Dick, pleased. 'Sort of thing we like. What do you say, Tim?'

'Woof,' said Tim, solemnly, bumping his tail to and fro across Dick's legs.

'And if we find there's absolutely nothing of interest, well, we can come back here with the things we've borrowed, and go on with our hike,' said Julian. 'But we'll have to sleep the night there because it will be dark by

It was a desolate ruin, blackened and scorched with fire

the time we've had a look round.'

They bought some loaves of bread, some butter and potted meat, and a big fruit cake. Also some more chocolate and some biscuits. Julian bought a bottle of orangeade as well.

'There's sure to be a well,' he said. 'Or a spring of some sort. We can dilute the orangeade and drink it when we're thirsty. Now I think we're ready. Come on!'

They couldn't go as fast as usual because they were carrying so many things. Timmy was the only one that ran as fast as ever – but then Timmy carried nothing but himself!

It was a really lovely walk over the moorlands. They climbed fairly high and had wonderful views all over the autumn country-side. They saw wild ponies again, in the distance this time, and a little herd

of dappled deer, that sped away immediately.

Julian was very careful to take the right paths – the ones traced so carefully on the map by the old man in the post-office. 'I expect he knew the way well because he was once a postman and had to take letters to Two-Trees!' said Dick, bending over the map. 'We're getting on, Ju – halfway there!'

The sun began to sink low. The children hurried as much as they could because once the sun had gone darkness would soon come. Fortunately the sky was very clear, so twilight would be later than it had been the night before.

'It looks as if the moorland near here gives way soon to a little bit of wooded country, according to the map,' said Julian. 'We'll look out for

clumps of trees.'

After another little stretch of moorland Julian pointed to the right. 'Look!' he said. 'Trees! Quite a lot – a proper little wood.'

'And isn't that water over there?' said Anne. They stood still and gazed hard. Was it Gloomy Water? It might be. It looked such a dark blue. They hurried on eagerly. It didn't look very far now. Timmy ran ahead, his long tail waving in the air.

They went down a little winding path and joined a cart-track that was very much overgrown – so overgrown that it hardly looked like a track. 'This must lead to Two-Trees,' said Julian. 'I wish the sun wasn't going down so quickly. We'll hardly have any time to look round!'

They entered a wood. The track wound through it. The trees must have been cleared at some time to make a road through the wood. And then, quite suddenly, they came on what had once been the lovely house of Two-Trees.

It was a desolate ruin, blackened and scorched with fire. The windows had no glass, the roof had gone, except for a few rafters here and there. Two birds flew up with a loud cry as the children went near.

'Two Maggies!' said Anne, with a laugh. They were black and white magpies, their long tails stretched out behind them. 'I wonder if they know the message too?'

The house stood on the edge of the lake. Gloomy Water was indeed a good name for it. It lay there, smooth and dark, a curious deep blue. No little waves lapped the edge. It was as still as if it were frozen.

'I don't like it,' said Anne. 'I don't like this place at all! I wish we hadn't come!'

Chapter 12

A Hiding Place at Two-Trees

NOBODY particularly liked the place. They all stared round and Julian pointed silently to something. At each end of the house was the great burnt trunk of a big tree.

'Those must be the two trees that gave the place its name,' said Julian. 'How horrid they look now, so stiff and black. Two-Trees and Gloomy Water – all so lonely and desolate now.'

The sun disappeared and a little chill came on the air. Julian suddenly became very busy. 'Come on – we must see if there's anywhere to shelter at all in this old ruin!'

They went to the silent house. The upper floors were all burnt out. The ground floor was pretty bad too, but Julian thought it might be possible to find a sheltered corner.

'This might do,' he said, coming out of a blackened room and beckoning the others to him. 'There is even a mouldy carpet still on the floor! And there's a big table. We could sleep under it if it rained – which I don't think it will do!'

'What a horrid room!' said Anne, looking round. 'I don't like its smell, either. I don't want to sleep here.'

'Well, find somewhere else then, but be quick about it,' said Julian. 'It will soon be dark. I'm going to collect heather and bracken straight away, before it's too dark. Coming, Dick and George?'

He went down the steps, Timmy just in front

The three of them went off and came back with vast armfuls of heather and brown bracken. Anne met them, looking excited.

'I've found somewhere. Somewhere much better than this horrid room. Come and look.'

She took them to what once had been the kitchen. A door lay flat on the floor at the end of the room, and a stone stairway led downwards.

'That leads down to the cellars,' said Anne. 'I came in here and saw that door. It was locked and I couldn't open it. Well, I tugged and tugged and the whole door came off its rusty old hinges and tumbled down almost on top of me! And I saw there were cellars down there!'

She stared at Julian beseechingly. 'They'll be dry. They won't be burnt and black like everywhere else. We'll be well-sheltered. Can't we sleep down there? I don't like the feel of these horrid burnt rooms.'

'It's an idea,' said Julian. He switched on his torch and let the beam light up the cellar below. It seemed spacious and smelt all right.

He went down the steps, Timmy just in front. He called up in surprise.

'There's a proper room down here, as well as cellars all round. Maybe it was a kind of sitting-room for the staff. It's wired for electricity too – they must have had their own electricity generator. Yes – we'll certainly come down here.'

It was a queer little room. Moth-eaten carpets were on the floor, and the furnishings were moth-eaten too and covered with dust. Spiders had been at work and George slashed fiercely at the long cobwebs that hung down and startled her by touching her face.

'There are still candles in the

candle-sticks on this shelf!' said Dick, surprised. 'We can light them and have a bit of brightness when it's dark. I must say I agree with Anne. There's something hateful about those burnt-out rooms.'

They piled heather and bracken into the cellar room on the floor. The furniture was so old and moth-eaten that it gave beneath their weight, and was useless for sitting on. The table was all right though. They soon set out their food on it after George had wiped it free of dust. She caused them all to have fits of choking because she was so vigorous in her dusting! They were driven up into the kitchen till the dust had settled.

It was dark outside now. The moon was not yet up. The wind rustled the dry leaves left on the trees around, but there was no lap-lap of water. The lake was as still as glass.

There was a cupboard in the cellar room. Julian opened it to see what was there. 'More

candles – good!' he said, bringing out a bundle. 'And plates and cups. Did anyone see a well outside? If so we could dilute some orangeade and have a drink with our supper.'

No one had noticed a well – but Anne suddenly remembered something queer she had seen in a corner of the kitchen, near the sink.

'I believe I saw a pump up there!' she said. 'Go and see, Ju. If so, it might still work.'

He went up the cellar-steps with a candle. Yes – Anne was right. That *was* an old pump over there in the corner. It probably pumped water into a tank and came out of the kitchen taps.

He turned on a big tap which was over the large sink. Then he took the handle of the pump and worked it vigorously up and down. Splash! Splash! Water came flooding through the big tap and splashed into the sink! That was good.

Julian pumped and pumped, feeling that he had better get rid of any water running into the tank for the first time for years. The tank might be dirty or rusty – he must wash it round with a good deal of pumped water first.

The water seemed to be clean and clear, and was certainly as cold as ice! Julian held a cup from the cellar cupboard under the tap, and then tasted the water. It was delicious.

'Good for you, Anne!' he called, going down the cellar-steps with a cupful of water, 'Dick, you find some more cups – or a jug or something in that cupboard, and we'll wash them out and fill them with water for our orangeade.'

The cellar room looked very cheerful as Julian came down

the steps. George and Anne had lighted six more candles, and stuck them about here and there. The light they gave was very pleasant, and they also warmed the room a little.

'Well, I suppose as usual, everyone wants a meal?' said Julian. 'Good thing we bought that bread and potted meat and stuff. I can't say I'm as hungry as I was at breakfast, but I'm getting that way.'

The four squatted round on their beds of heather and bracken. They had put down their ground-sheets first in case the floor was damp, though it didn't seem to be. Over bread and butter and potted meat they discussed their plans. They would sleep there for the night and then have all the next day to examine Two-Trees and the lake.

'What exactly are we looking for?' asked Anne. 'Do you suppose there's some secret here, Julian?'

'Yes,' said Julian. 'And I think I know what it is!'

'What?' asked George and Anne, surprised. Dick thought he knew. Julian explained.

'Well, we know that a prisoner called Nailer sent an important message by his escaped friend to two people – one he wanted to send to Dirty Dick – but he didn't get it – and the other to Maggie, whoever she is. Now what secret does he want to tell them?'

'I think I can guess,' said Dick. 'But go on.'

'Now suppose that Nailer has done some big robberies,' said Julian. 'I don't know what. Jewellery robberies probably, because they are the commonest with big criminals. All right – he does a big robbery – he hides the stuff till he hopes the hue and cry will be over – but he's caught and put into prison for a number of years. But he doesn't tell where the stuff is hidden! He daren't even write a letter to tell his friends outside the prison where it is. All his letters are read before they leave the prison. So what is he to do?'

'Wait till someone escapes and then give him a message,' said Dick. 'And that's just what happened, isn't it, Julian? That round-headed man I saw was the escaped prisoner, and he was sent to tell Dirty Dick and Maggie where the stolen goods were hidden – so that they could get them before anyone else did!'

'Yes, I'm sure that's it,' said Julian. 'His friend, the escaped prisoner, probably wouldn't understand the message at all – but Dirty Dick and Maggie would, because they knew all about the robbery. And now Maggie will certainly try to find out where the stuff is.'

'Well, we must find it first!' said George, her eyes gleaming

with excitement. 'We're here first, anyway. And tomorrow, as early as possible we'll begin to snoop round. What was the next clue in the message, Dick? After Two-Trees and Gloomy Water.'

'Saucy Jane,' said Dick.

'Sounds a silly sort of clue,' said Anne. 'Do you suppose Maggie and Jane are *both* in the secret?'

'Saucy Jane sounds more like a boat to me,' said Dick.

'Of *course*!' said George. 'A boat! Why not? There's a lake

Now it was whole again. They all examined it carefully

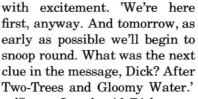

here, and I imagine that people don't build a house beside a lake unless they want to go boating and bathing and fishing. I bet we shall find a boat called Saucy Jane tomorrow – and the stolen goods will be inside it.'

'Too easy!' said Dick. 'And not a very clever place either. Anyone could come across goods hidden in a boat. No – Saucy Jane is a clue, but we shan't find the stolen goods in her. And remember, there's that bit of paper as well. It must have something to do with the hiding-place too, I should think.'

'Where is it?' asked Julian. 'That wretched policeman! He tore it up. Have you still got the pieces, Dick?'

'Of course,' said Dick. He fished in his pocket and brought them out. 'Four little pieces! Anyone got some gummed paper?'

Nobody had – but George produced a small roll of Elastoplast. Strips were cut and stuck behind the four portions of paper. Now it was whole again. They all examined it carefully.

'Look – four lines drawn, meeting in the centre,' said Julian. 'At the outer end of each line there's a word, so faintly written I can hardly read one of them. What's this one? "Tock Hill". And this next one is "Steeple". Whatever are the others?'

They made them out at last. '"Chimney",' said Anne. 'That's the third.'

'And "Tall Stone" is the fourth,' said George. 'Whatever do they all mean? We shall never, never find out!'

'We'll sleep on it,' said Julian, cheerfully. 'It's wonderful what good ideas come in the night. It will be a very interesting little problem to solve tomorrow in the daylight!'

Chapter 13

A Night in the Cellar

This was better than last night when she was all alone in that horrid little loft

THE piece of paper was carefully folded and this time Julian took it for safe keeping. 'I can't imagine what it means, but it's clearly important,' he said. 'We may quite suddenly come on something – or think of something – that will give us a clue to what the words and the lines mean on the paper.'

'We mustn't forget that dear Maggie has a copy of the paper too,' said Dick. 'She probably knows better than we do what it all means!'

'If she does, she will pay a visit to Two-Trees too,' said Anne. 'We ought to keep a look-out for her. Should we have to hide if we saw her?'

Julian considered this. 'No,' he said, 'I certainly don't think we should hide. Maggie can't *possibly* guess that we have had the message from Nailer, and the paper too. We had better just say we are on a hike and found this place and thought we would shelter here. All perfectly true.'

'And we can keep an eye on her, and see what she does if she comes!' said Dick, with a grin. 'Won't she be annoyed!'

'She wouldn't come alone,' said Julian, thoughtfully. 'I should think it quite likely that she would come with Dirty Dick! He didn't get the message, but she did – and probably part of her message was the statement that Dirty Dick would know everything too. So she would get in touch with him.'

'Yes – and be surprised that he hadn't got the message or the paper,' said George. 'Still, they'd think that the escaped fellow hadn't been able to get to Dirty Dick.'

'All very complicated,' said Anne, yawning. 'I can't follow any more arguments and explanations – I'm half asleep. How long are you going to be before you settle down?'

Dick yawned too. 'I'm coming now,' he said. 'My bed of bracken and heather looks inviting. It's not at all cold in here, is it?'

'The only thing I don't like is the thought of those cellars beyond this little underground room,' said Anne. 'I keep thinking that Maggie and her friends might be there, waiting to pounce on us when we are asleep.'

'You're silly,' said George, scornfully. '*Really* silly! Do you honestly suppose that Timmy would lie here quietly if there was anyone in those cellars? You know jolly well he would be barking his head off!'

'Yes, I know all that,' said Anne, snuggling down in her heathery bed. 'It's just my imagination. You haven't got any, George, so you don't bother about imaginary fears. I'm not *really* scared while Timmy is here. But I do think it's funny the way we always plunge into something peculiar when we're together.'

'Adventures always do come to some people,' said Dick. 'You've only got to read the lives of explorers and see how they simply *walk* into adventures all the time.'

'Yes, but I'm not an explorer,' said Anne. 'I'm an ordinary person, and I'd be just as pleased if things *didn't* keep happening to me.'

The others laughed. 'I don't expect anything much will happen,' said Julian, comfortingly. 'We go back to school on Tuesday and that's not far off. Not much time for anything to happen!'

He was wrong of course. Things can happen one after the other in a few minutes! Still, Anne cuddled down feeling happier. This was better than last night when she was all alone in that horrid little loft. Now she had all the others with her, Timmy too.

Anne and George had one big bed between them. They drew their two rugs over themselves, and put their blazers on top too. Nobody had undressed because Julian had said that they might be too cold in just their night things.

Timmy as usual put himself on George's feet. She moved them because he was heavy. He wormed his way up the bed and found a very comfortable place between the knees of the two girls. He gave a heavy sigh.

'That means he's planning to go to sleep!' said George. 'Are you quite comfortable, Anne?'

'Yes,' said Anne, sleepily. 'I like Timmy there. I feel safe!'

Julian was blowing out the candles. He left just one burning. Then he got into his bed of bracken and heather beside Dick. He felt tired too.

The four slept like logs. Nobody moved except Timmy, who got up once or twice in the night and sniffed round inquiringly. He had heard a noise in the cellars. He stood at the closed door that led to the cellars and listened, his head on one side.

He sniffed at the crack. Then he went back to bed, satisfied. It was only a toad! Timmy knew the smell of toads. If toads liked to crawl about in the night, they were welcome to!

The second time he awoke he thought he heard something up in the kitchen above. He padded up the steps, his paws making a click-click-click as he went. He stood in the kitchen silently, his eyes gleaming like green lamps, as the moon shone on him.

An animal with a long bushy tail began to slink away outside the house. It was a fine fox. It had smelt unusual smells near the old ruin – the scent of people

An animal with a long bushy tail began to slink away outside the house

and of a dog, and it had come to find out what was happening.

It had slunk into the kitchen and then smelt the strong scent of Timmy in the room below. As quietly as a cat it had slunk out again – but Timmy had awakened!

Now the dog stood watching and waiting – but the fox had gone! Timmy sniffed its scent and padded to the door. He debated whether to bark and go after the fox.

The scent grew very faint, and Timmy decided not to make a fuss. He padded back to the steps that led down to the cellar room, and curled up on George's feet again. He was very heavy, but George was too tired to wake up and push him off. Timmy lay with one ear cocked for a while, and then went to sleep again, with his ear still cocked. He was a good sentinel!

It was dark in the cellar when the one candle went out. There was no daylight or sunshine to wake the children down in that dim little room, and they slept late.

Julian woke up first. He found his bed suddenly very hard, and he turned over to find a comfortable place. The heather and bracken had been flattened with his weight, and the floor below was very hard indeed! The movement woke him up, and he lay blinking in the darkness. Where was he?

He remembered at once and sat up. Dick woke too and yawned. 'Dick! It's half-past eight!' said Julian, looking at the luminous hands of his wristwatch. 'We've slept for hours and hours!'

They rolled out of their heathery bed. Timmy leapt off George's feet and came over to them, his tail wagging gladly.

He had been half-awake for a long time and was very glad to see Julian and Dick awake too, because he was thirsty.

The girls awoke – and soon there was a great deal of noise and activity going on. Anne and George washed at the big stone sink, the cold water making them squeal. Timmy lapped up a big bowlful of water gladly. The boys debated whether or not to have a splash in the lake. They felt very dirty.

Dick shivered at the thought. 'Still, I think we ought to,' he said. 'Come on, Ju!'

The two boys went down to the lake-side and leapt in. It was icy-cold! They struck out strongly and came back glowing and shouting.

By the time they were back the girls had got breakfast in the cellar room. It was darker than the kitchen, but all of them disliked the look of the burnt, scorched rooms above. The bread and butter, potted meat, cake and chocolate went down well.

In the middle of the meal a sound came echoing into the old house – bells! Anne stopped eating, and her heart beat fast.

But they were not the clanging warning bells she had heard before!

'Church bells,' said Julian at once, seeing Anne's sudden look of fright. 'Lovely sound I always think!'

'Oh, *yes*,' said Anne, thankfully. 'So it is. It's Sunday and people are going to church. I'd like to go too, on this lovely sunny October day.'

'We might walk across the moor to the nearest village if you like,' said Dick, looking at his watch. 'But we should be very late.'

It was decided that it was much too late so they planned what to do that day.

'The first thing, of course, is to see if there's a boathouse and find out if there's a boat called *Saucy Jane*,' said Julian. 'Then we'd better try and puzzle out what that plan means. We could wander here and there and see if we can find Tall Stone – and I'll look at the map to see if Tock Hill is marked.'

'You boys go and get some heather and bracken while we clear away and wash up,' said Anne. 'That is if you mean us to camp here another night.'

'Yes. I think we will,' said Julian. 'I think we may find things rather interesting here this week-end!'

Julian went out with Dick and they brought in a great deal more bedding. Everyone had complained that the hard floor came through the amount of heather and bracken they had used the night before, and poor George was quite stiff.

The girls took the dirty things up to the big sink to wash them. There was nothing to dry them with so they laid them on the old draining board to dry.

They wiped their hands on their hankies and then felt ready for exploring round outside. With Timmy bounding here and there they went down to the lake. A path had once led down to it, with a low wall on each side. But now the wall was broken, moss had crept everywhere, and the path was choked with tufts of heather and even with small bushes of gorse.

The lake was still and dark. Some moorhens chugged across it quickly, disappearing under the water when they saw the children.

'Now, what about that boathouse?' said Dick at last. 'Is there one – or not?'

Chapter 14

Where is the Saucy Jane?

WORDS can give us lots of fun. We can hide words in sentences, change one word into another, use words for codes and quizzes, and so on. Here are a few examples for you to puzzle over. The answers will be found on page 78, but try not to look at them unless you are well and truly 'lost for words'!

FUN WITH WORDS

1. Changelings

You are asked to change one word into another. You can only change one letter on each line, and each line must give a word to be found in a dictionary. Here is an example to give you the idea – how to change BOOT into SHOE:

       BOOT
       SOOT
       SHOT
       SHOE

Now see if you can change LAND into SEAS, SMOKE into FLAME and HEAD into FOOT.

2. A Lady in Hiding

In the letter-square below are hidden three words which make up the name of a lady in a well-known nursery rhyme. You can find her name by starting at the correct letter and moving on to any one of the next nearest letters (above, below, across or diagonally) until all the 16 letters have been used up. No letter can be used more than once. We'll let you into a secret – the starting point is at one of the two letter O's.

       R A B H
       D B R U
       D O O E
       L M T H

3. The 'Shorthand' Messages

Here are two messages written in what seems to be a curious kind of shorthand. Can you make them into sensible sentences?

(a)

STAND	TAKE	TO	TAKING
I	U	THROW	MY

(b)

       manager   Mr.
       interviewed 45 noon yesterday
       The   20 cwt.

4. A Shortage of E's

A printer wanted to set up a sentence in type, but found that he had run out of the letter E. He set up the rest of the letters in the sentence and went off to find a supply of the letter E. Below, you see the letters he set up.

Can you put the missing E's in their correct places and then separate the letters into words to make a sentence about a particular kind of bird?

THAGLISXPCTDTOBCOM-
VRYRARINDD

5. An Old Map

The other day we came across a much-worn map of the world. Some of the letters of the names of countries were worn off. Can you replace the missing letters to complete the names of the ten countries below?

1. – – L – S
2. C – – N –
3. D – NM – – –
4. – N – D –
5. – G – P –
6. – – RW – Y
– – – EE – E
8. A – A – – A
9. – – ST – A – – A
10. C – – L – N

6. Hidden Creatures

In each of the sentences below is hidden the name of an animal, a bird or a fish. Can you spot them?
1. They both rushed out of the room.
2. Is there a bench or seat where I can rest?
3. The message was in code.
4. "Let's go outside, Eric."
5. She lobs terribly at tennis.
6. Eli only had one friend.

Answers on page 78

The Badger

TIMMY, the Five's faithful dog, delighted in chasing rabbits (not that he ever caught one!) but he took jolly good care to steer clear of badgers. No wild animal in Britain will pick a quarrel with Brock. Despite his size and weight, he is very quick and nimble. What is more, his very powerful jaws and teeth can inflict terrible wounds.

It is only when they are cornered and on the defensive that badgers become dangerous. Normally they are peaceful and harmless, and will vanish in a flash if their keen sense of smell tells them that humans are around. Their sense of hearing is very keen, too.

In many ways badgers are almost human. They remain faithful to one mate, and they are sticklers for cleanliness. Not only do they keep themselves clean, but they keep their underground tunnels (called setts) free of all rubbish. A fox will allow the remains of its meals to accumulate and rot in its 'earth', but not so Brock.

Any soiled bedding is replaced by new, and even young cubs are taught that they must use the specially dug 'toilets' outside the sett!

The word badger is believed to come from a French word *bêcheur,* meaning digger. And what an amazing digger Brock is! He is built for the job – sturdy leg bones with specially strengthened ankle joints, and long, sharp and very strong claws (he sharpens them regularly on tree trunks).

Selecting a spot (often on a sloping bank), he will tunnel out a ton of soil with incredible speed. Large stones are loosened and bulldozed out of the tunnel as though some mechanical excavator were at work. Setts can be very extensive indeed, consisting of over a hundred yards of tunnel with several entrances. Brock thinks of ventilation, too, digging ventilation shafts up to the surface at intervals.

Some naturalists believe that when a badger dies at the end of a tunnel it is walled up by the other badgers. But one famous naturalist has witnessed the amazing sight of a badger 'funeral'. A sow badger dragged her dead mate out of the sett, dug a deep hole and, with the help of another badger, pushed the body into it and covered it with soil!

Badgers are largely creatures of the night, and because of their keen sense of smell and hearing they are very seldom seen by the average countryman.

If you want to see a badger, you will first have to find its sett. The entrance hole is three or four times larger than that of a rabbit burrow, but the chief clue to look for is the pile of earth thrown out during Brock's tunnelling operations. Actually, there will probably be several entrances. To find out which entrance is in use, either look for Brock's five-toed footprints in the excavated soil, or fix thin sticks across the entrances several hours before you take up your position. The tunnel with the sticks displaced will be the one to watch.

You should be in position very soon after sunset. Be sure to stand where the wind will blow your scent away from Brock's front door. If you can find a convenient tree to perch in, so much the better. Badgers have poor sight, but you must keep absolutely silent. If the night is really dark, how can we see our quarry? The answer is to use a torch masked by red paper. For some reason, red light doesn't seem to worry Brock in the slightest!

If your luck is in, you will first hear the chink of loose stones at the entrance of the sett, and probably a few faint pig-like grunts. Brock never comes straight out. First he sticks his white-striped snout out of the tunnel and scents the air for possible danger. If he is satisfied, he will scramble up on to the 'door-step' of his sett, then wander around nosing about in the dead leaves and undergrowth in search of worms, slugs, snails and similar tit-bits. Very often he will spend a little time sharpening his claws on a tree trunk.

The cubs – two or three in a litter – are usually born during February and early March. If your badger-watching is done between April and early summer, you stand a good chance of seeing the cubs at play. It is fascinating to watch. They squeal, fight and jump about with great gusto, and Mum often joins in as well. The sow also begins to teach them how to fetch bedding material, dig tunnels and hunt for their own food.

What do badgers eat? It's a lengthy menu! Worms seem to be their favourite food, but they eat grubs of all kinds, rats, mice, shrews, hedgehogs and even young rabbits. Roots and bluebell bulbs are always welcome, and fat tender buds in spring. In autumn they eat lots of blackberries, apples and acorns.

Some farmers accuse badgers of killing lambs and poultry, but they have to be very hard-pressed for food before they do so. It is quite probable that Brock is often blamed for a fox's 'crimes'. The majority of naturalists believe that badgers do far more good than harm.

Creatures of the

ABOUT the time we humans are preparing for bed, nature's night prowlers are bestirring themselves and setting out on their various 'breakfast' trails. Being so keen on hiking, camping and other outdoor activities, Julian and the rest of the Five knew quite a lot about the ways of the wild night.

One night, instead of creeping into bed, how about asking a local naturalist to take you on an after-dark excursion into the countryside in the hope of getting a glimpse of one or other of nature's 'night shift' creatures? There are naturalist groups of one sort or another in almost every town and you should have no difficulty in getting things organised.

Apart from badgers and foxes (which you can read about on other pages) you may be lucky enough to see quite a number of other creatures seldom seen in the daytime.

One of the first things you will notice is that the so-called 'silent' night is anything but silent! Apart from the eerie call of the owls, we hear mysterious rustlings in the undergrowth, the snapping of twigs, or the startled cry of some luckless creature caught unawares by some rival night prowler.

If your excursion is during the warmer months of the year you are pretty certain to see a few bats. There are twenty species in Britain, most of them being found in the southern counties of England.

The bat is a strange creature in many ways. It is the only mammal able to fly; it has wings like a bird but fur like an animal; although it looks like a bird, it makes no nest and lays no eggs, but gives birth to its young like an animal. Even in summer a resting bat is usually quite cold, and before it can take-off in flight it has to 'rev-up' by shivering quite violently in order to raise its body temperature!

The fact that a bat can lower its body temperature for long periods has the effect of giving it a long life. Small bats live up to twenty years.

Bats are not blind, as some people imagine, but at night their sight is very poor indeed. Yet at night we see them darting about at great speed, never colliding with each other or with any obstacle in their flight path.

The answer to the riddle is 'bat radar' or echo-location. When in flight, a bat produces a steady stream of high-pitched sounds. The bat's supersensitive ears detect the echoes when the sounds are reflected by obstacles ahead. In this amazing manner a bat is able to navigate by sound, not sight!

With ordinary luck we should see a hedgehog – perhaps a whole family – nosing their way through the undergrowth like miniature tanks in search of worms, beetles, slugs and other tasty morsels. That they are so plentiful is due to the fact that they have few enemies.

You may think them slow-moving and clumsy, but actually they can run quite swiftly when necessary, and they can jump at least a foot into the air. They can climb over fences and sometimes high into trees. If they are at the top of a steeply sloping bank they will sometimes curl themselves into a ball and roll down the slope.

Hedgehogs must often come face to face with adders, but that doesn't worry them. Snake-bites don't harm them and they are immune to all but a very few other poisons. Never drive hedgehogs from your garden for they do a fine job gobbling up garden pests.

If you switch on your torch in the middle of a wood it is quite likely that, before long, an owl will appear on the scene, as they are very inquisitive birds. You won't hear it come because it is almost silent in flight.

'Wise as an owl' is a well-known saying. With its large ears and eyes it certainly *looks* wise, but naturalists say it is far less intelligent than a crow or a

Night

magpie. Mother Nature has seen to it that owls are well equipped to be hunters of the night. Their great ears can detect the faintest rustle in the undergrowth from a considerable distance; and their huge eyes are specially designed for seeing in the dark.

A naturalist once decided to test an owl's power of sight and hearing. He buried himself in a mound of hay, poked one finger out of the top and wiggled it. He wished he hadn't thought of the idea, for an owl swooped down and gave his finger a nasty gash with its sharp talons!

There's no telling what you may see, or hear, in the countryside after dark. If it is April or May you may hear the thrilling song of the nightingale; in winter, the bark of a fox or the scream of a vixen. Or, with lots of luck, you may have the rare experience of watching a moonlight display of aquabatics by a family of otters.

Bryn Gwynant Youth Hostel in the Welsh mountains

Colour transparency by Frank Slater

Youth Hostelling is Fun

THE Five liked nothing better than packing their rucksacks and setting out to explore the countryside. There are so many interesting things to be seen and places to be visited that as soon as one trip was over they were planning the next.

One of the best and cheapest ways of exploring this lovely old country of ours is to become a member of the Youth Hostels Association. It was started in 1930 to enable young people to enjoy the delights of the countryside at much less cost than would otherwise be the case.

Actually, the title, Youth Hostels Association, is a trifle misleading, for membership is open to anyone from the age of five years upwards. If you are under the age of twelve years, however, you can only stay at a hostel if accompanied by a parent or some responsible person.

There are 260 hostels in England and Wales, 150 in Scotland and Ireland, nearly 3,000 on the Continent of Europe, plus a great many more in over 50 countries. Hostels are *not* hotels! They are places where you can

stay overnight in the best of good company and be on your way again the next morning. Or, if you wish to use the hostel as a centre for exploring a particular area of countryside, you are allowed to use the hostel for not more than three nights in succession. As a rule, the hostels are closed from 10 a.m. until 5 p.m.

One of the reasons why hostelling charges are so low is that the Y.H.A. is not out to make profit. People who use the hostels are expected to lend a hand with the daily chores and this helps to keep costs down.

Not the least exciting part of hostelling are the hostels themselves. Some have only a few beds and others as many as 200. Some have been specially built and others are centuries old. At the end of the day when you head for the next hostel you may find it anything from a shepherd's hut or a country cottage to a genuine old Norman castle, complete with dungeons!

Hostels may differ as buildings, but they all have this in common: they provide simple but adequate accommodation, a common room and a kitchen where members may cook their own meals if they wish. At many hostels, however, you can obtain meals cooked by the Warden in charge.

What about those chores we mentioned? With everybody lending a hand, these are soon done.

After supper (you can cook your own if you wish) you'll probably feel like taking things easy in the common room. Here you can often sit round a blazing log fire and exchange travellers' tales with your fellow hostellers. This is one of the joys of being a member of the Y.H.A. There are no barriers of race or colour, so your fireside companions may be a party of students from the U.S.A., a family from Australia exploring historic places in the 'Old Country', Scouts or Guides on a winter hike, or perhaps a group of bird-watching enthusiasts. Old hands are always willing to help those who are new to hostelling and the Warden is a mine of information on routes and places of interest in the locality.

Those with enough energy left after the day's adventures can enjoy a game of table tennis or darts, but soon after 10 p.m. the Warden will remind us that it will soon be time for bed, and everyone is expected to observe the 'lights out' rule, usually about 10.30 p.m.

Unlike campers, youth hostellers do not need to carry all their bedding around. The hostels provide bed, mattress, pillow and blankets, and you can hire a sheet sleeping bag of the type approved by the Y.H.A., from the Warden for 30p plus V.A.T.

Actually, providing the traveller with food and shelter is not the only service the Y.H.A. provides. Every year it organises a wide variety of 'Adventure' holidays for boys and girls in the 11 to 15 age group, and for older members of 16 years and upwards.

You can take your choice from exciting activities such as dinghy sailing, canoeing, underwater swimming, walking, bird-watching, geology, cycling, brass-rubbing, painting and sketching, pony trekking, rock climbing and mountaincraft, photography, fishing or fossil-hunting. Or you can have the thrill of a seven-day holiday by horse-drawn narrow boat through England's canals.

There are also Continental walking holiday tours for boys and girls aged 13-15 years.

By the way, if you become a member of the Y.H.A., your membership card will entitle you to use hostels in more than forty countries!

A recent addition to the facilities offered by the Y.H.A. is the Hub of England Cycle Hire Scheme, planned by the Countryside Commission, the Cyclists' Touring Club and the Y.H.A. For a small charge, cycles can be hired from five hostels so that Y.H.A. members can explore the villages and countryside around the centre of England.

The five hostels from which cycles can be hired are: Badby (Northants), Greens Norton (Northants), Charlbury (Oxon), Inglesham (Wilts) and Duntisbourne Abbots (Glos).

What does it cost to become one of the quarter of a million youth hostellers in Britain? At the time of writing, membership fees are as follows: Young (age 5-15) 75p per year; Junior (age 16-20) £1.40; Senior (21 years and over) £2.00.

Hostels vary so greatly in type that they have been sorted out into four grades – Simple, Standard, Superior and Special. Charges for staying at a Simple grade hostel for one night are (Young) 50p; (Junior) 65p; (Senior) 75p. Charges at a Standard hostel are slightly higher – 65p, 80p and 90p.

At most hostels, hot meals can be supplied by the Warden. Supper costs 80p and breakfast 65p. Packed lunches to take on your travels cost 40p.

Many of the hostels have a store where you can buy your own food and so enable you to prepare simple meals in the hostel kitchen.

If you would like to join in the fun of hostelling, write for further details and an enrolment form. The address is:

Y.H.A. National Office,

Trevelyan House,

8 St. Stephens Hill,

St. Albans, Herts AL1 2DY

In these days of rising costs, the Y.H.A. is still able to offer you bargain price holidays – and in good company, too!

By the way, we guess that Timmy is not at all keen on the Y.H.A. idea, for animals, alas, are not allowed in hostels or hostel grounds!

69

Chapter 15
Maggie and Dirty Dick

HAVING SEARCHED FOR THE **SAUCY JANE** IN THE BOAT-HOUSE NEAR 'TWO-TREES' WITHOUT SUCCESS, THE FIVE SET ABOUT EXPLORING THE SHORE-LINE AROUND GLOOMY WATER. BUT BRAMBLES FORCED A RETREAT — AND JUST AS THEY WERE ABOUT TO RETURN TO THE BOAT-HOUSE FOR THE RAFT, MAGGIE AND DIRTY DICK TURNED UP...

SO THAT'S MAGGIE. DON'T LIKE THE LOOK OF HER — SHE LOOKS AS HARD AS NAILS...

LISTEN, DON'T TURN A HAIR. WE'LL JUST WALK RIGHT OUT INTO THE OPEN, CHATTERING AWAY TOGETHER. LET THEM THINK WE'RE A BUNCH OF HARMLESS KIDS, OKAY? AND LEAVE ANY LEADING QUESTIONS TO ME. READY?

HERE WE ARE AGAIN — THERE'S THE OLD HOUSE! MY WORD, IT LOOKS WORSE THAN EVER THIS MORNING!

'ELLO — TROUBLE!

WHO ARE YOU? WHAT ARE YOU DOING HERE? DON'T YOU KNOW THIS IS PRIVATE PROPERTY?

WE'RE HIKING... ANYWAY, THIS ISN'T PRIVATE LAND — IT'S ONLY A RUIN. ANYONE CAN COME. WE WANT TO EXPLORE THIS LAKE — IT LOOKS EXCITING.

YOU CAN'T EXPLORE THIS LAKE, IT'S DANGEROUS. PEOPLE ARE FORBIDDEN TO BATHE IN IT OR USE A BOAT ON IT.

FUNNY, WE WEREN'T TOLD THAT. IN FACT, WE WERE TOLD HOW TO GET HERE. NO ONE SAID THE LAKE WAS FORBIDDEN. YOU'VE BEEN TOLD WRONGLY.

ANNE, GEORGE AND DICK CHIPPED IN WITH THEIR OWN LINE OF DEFENCE...

WE WANT TO WATCH THE MOOR-HENS, YOU SEE. WE'RE FOND OF NATURE...

AND WE'VE BEEN TOLD THERE ARE DEER NEAR HERE...

AND WILD PONIES. WE SAW SOME YESTERDAY. THEY WERE REALLY LOVELY. HAVE YOU SEEN ANY?

BUT THE FRIENDS' CHATTER ONLY MADE DIRTY DICK MORE IRRITABLE...

STOP THIS NONSENSE! PEOPLE AREN'T ALLOWED HERE! NOW YOU CLEAR OFF BEFORE I MAKE YOU!

TIMMY!

72

Chapter 16

Out on the Raft

THERE were four little paddles. Dick got them, and gave everyone one each. Timmy looked down solemnly at the raft. What was it? Surely he was not expected to ride on that bobbing, floating thing?

Julian was on the raft already, holding it steady for the others. He helped Anne on and then George stepped down. Dick clambered on last – well, not quite last, because Timmy was not yet on.

'Come on, Tim!' said George. 'It's all right! It's not the kind of boat you're used to, but it acts in the same way. Come *on*, Timmy!'

Timmy jumped down and the raft bobbed violently. Anne sat down suddenly with a giggle. 'Oh dear – Timmy is so *sudden*! Keep still, Tim – there isn't enough room on this raft for you to walk all over it.'

Julian pushed the raft out of the boat-house. It knocked against the wooden ledge as it

went, and then swung out on to the backwater outside. It floated very smoothly.

'Here we go!' said Julian, paddling deftly. 'I'll steer, Dick. None of you need to paddle till I say so. I can paddle and steer at the moment, till we get on to the lake itself.'

They were all sitting on the raft except Timmy, who was standing up. He was very interested in seeing the water flow past so quickly. *Was* this a boat then? He was used to boats – but in boats the water was never quite so near. Timmy put out a paw into the water. It was pleasantly cool and tickled him. He lay down with his nose almost in the water.

'You're a funny dog, Timmy!' said Anne. 'You won't get up too suddenly, will you, or you'll knock me overboard.'

Julian paddled down the little backwater and the raft swung out on to the lake itself. The

children looked to see if there was any sign of Maggie and Dirty Dick.

'There they are!' said Julian. 'Out in the middle, rowing hard. Shall we follow them? If they know where the *Saucy Jane* is they'll lead us to it.'

'Yes. Follow them,' said Dick. 'Shall *we* paddle now? We'll have to be quick or we may lose them.'

They all paddled hard, and the raft suddenly swung to and fro in a most alarming manner.

'Hey, stop!' shouted Julian. 'You're all paddling against one another. We're going round in circles. Dick and Anne go one side and George the other. That's better. Watch how we're going, all of you, and stop paddling for a moment if the raft swings round too much.'

They soon got into the way of paddling so that the raft went straight ahead. It was great fun. They got very hot and wished they could ake off their thick

73

jerseys. The sun was quite warm, and there was no wind at all – it was really a perfect October afternoon.

'They've stopped rowing,' said George, suddenly. 'They're looking at something – do you suppose they have got a bit of paper like the one we have, with the same marks, and are examining it? I *wish* I could see!'

They all stopped paddling and looked towards the boat in which Maggie and Dirty Dick sat. They were certainly examining something very carefully – their heads were close together. But they were too far away for the children to see if they were holding a piece of paper.

'Come on – we'll get as close to them as we can!' said Julian, beginning to paddle again. 'I expect it will make them absolutely mad to see us so close, but we can't help that!'

They paddled hard again, and at last came up to the boat. Timmy barked. Maggie and Dirty Dick at once looked round and saw the raft and the four children. They stared at them savagely.

'Hallo!' cried Dick, waving a paddle. 'We took the raft out. It goes well. Does your boat go all right?'

Maggie went red with rage. 'You'll get into trouble for taking that raft without permission,' she shouted.

'Whose permission did *you* ask when you took that boat?' shouted back Julian. 'Tell us and we'll ask their permission to use this raft!'

George laughed. Maggie scowled, and Dirty Dick looked as if he would like to throw his oars at them.

'Keep away from us!' he shouted. 'We don't want you kids spoiling our afternoon!'

'We like to be friendly!' called Dick, and made George laugh again.

Maggie and Dirty Dick had a hurried and angry conversation. They glared at the raft and then Maggie gave an order to Dirty Dick. He took up the oars again, and began to row, looking rather mutinous.

'Come on – follow,' said Julian, so the four began to paddle again following after the boat. 'Maybe we'll learn something now.'

But they didn't. Dirty Dick rowed the boat towards the west bank, and the raft followed. Then he swung out into the middle again, and again the raft followed, the children panting in their efforts to keep up.

Dirty Dick rowed right across to the east bank and stayed there till the children came up. Then he rowed off again.

'Having some nice exercise, aren't you?' called the woman in her harsh voice. 'So good for you all!'

The boat swung out to the middle of the lake again. Dick groaned. 'Blow! My arms are so tired I can hardly paddle. What are they doing?'

'I'm afraid they're just leading us on a wild goose chase,' said Julian, ruefully. 'They have evidently made up their minds that they won't look for the *Saucy Jane* while we're about – they're just tiring us out!'

'Well, if *that's* what they're doing I'm not playing!' said Dick, and he put down his paddle and lay flat on his back, his knees drawn up, panting hard.

The others did the same. They were all tired. Timmy licked each one sympathetically and then sat down on George. She pushed him off so violently that he nearly fell into the water.

'Timmy! Right on my middle!' cried George, surprised and indignant. 'You great clumsy dog, you!'

Timmy licked her all over, shocked at being scolded by George. She was too exhausted to push him away.

'What's happened to the boat?' asked Anne at last. 'I'm too tired to sit up and see.'

Julian sat up, groaning. 'Oh my back! Now where is that wretched boat? Oh, there it is – right away down the lake, making for the landing-place by the house – or for the boat-house probably. They've given up the search for the *Saucy Jane* for the time being anyway.'

'Thank goodness,' said Anne. 'Perhaps we can give it up too – till tomorrow anyhow! Stop snuffling down my neck, Timmy. What do you want us to do, Julian.'

'I think we'd better get back,' said Julian. 'It's too late now to start searching the banks of the lake – and anyway somehow I think it wouldn't be much use. The two in the boat didn't appear to be going anywhere near the banks – except when they began to play that trick on us to make us tired out!'

'Well, let's get back then,' said George. 'But I simply must have a rest first. Timmy, I shall push you into the water if you keep sitting on my legs.'

There was a sudden splash. George sat up in alarm. Timmy was not on the raft!

He was swimming in the water, looking very pleased with himself.

'There! He thought he'd rather jump in than be pushed,' said Dick, grinning at George.

'*You* pushed him in!' said George, looking fierce.

'I didn't,' said Dick. 'He just

took a header. He's having a jolly good time. I say – what about putting a rope round him and getting him to pull us to shore? It would save an awful lot of paddling.'

George was just about to say what she thought of *that* idea, when she caught Dick's sly grin. She kicked out at him.

'Don't keep baiting me, Dick. I'll push *you* in, in a minute.'

'Like to try?' asked Dick, at once. 'Come on. I'd like a wrestle to see who'd go into the water first.'

George, of course, always rose to a challenge. She never could resist one. She was up in a moment and fell on Dick, who nearly went overboard at once.

'Shut up, you two!' said Julian, crossly. 'We haven't got a change of clothing, you know that. And I don't want to take you back with bronchitis or pneumonia. Stop it, George.'

George recognized the tone in his voice and she stopped. She ran her hand through her short curls and gave a sudden grin.

'All right, Teacher!' she said, and sat down meekly. She picked up her paddle.

Julian picked up his. 'We'll get

On a high slope about a mile away she saw something that interested her

back,' he said. 'The sun's sinking low. It seems to slide down the sky at a most remarkable speed in October.'

They took a very wet Timmy on board and began to paddle back. Anne thought it was a truly lovely evening. She gazed dreamily round as she paddled. The lake was a wonderful dark blue, and the ripples they made turned to silver as they ran away from the raft. Two moorhens said 'crek-crek' and swam round the raft in curiosity, their heads bobbing like clockwork.

Anne gazed over the tops of the trees that grew at the lakeside. The sky was turning pink. Away in the distance, on a high slope about a mile away she saw something that interested her.

It looked like a high stone. She pointed at it. 'Look, Julian,' she said. 'What's that stone? Is it a boundary mark, or something? It must be very big.'

Julian looked where she was pointing. 'Where?' he said. 'Oh,

that. I can't imagine what it is.'

'It looks like a very tall stone,' said Dick, suddenly catching sight of it too.

'A tall stone,' repeated Anne, wondering where she had heard that before. 'A tall . . . oh, of *course*! It was printed on that plan, wasn't it – on the piece of paper Dick was given. Tall Stone! Don't you remember?'

'Yes. So it was,' said Dick and he stared at the faraway stone monument with interest. Then as the raft swung onwards, high trees hid the stone. It was gone.

'Tall Stone,' said Julian. 'It may be only a coincidence, of course. It wants a bit of thinking about, though. Funny we should suddenly spot it.'

'Would the loot be buried there?' asked George, doubtfully. Julian shook his head. 'Oh, no,' he said, 'it is probably hidden in some position explained by that mysterious map. Paddle up, everyone! We really must get back.'

Chapter 17

Tit for Tat

WHEN they arrived at the boat-house there was no sign of Maggie or Dick. But their boat was in the shed, tied up in front of the other two, where it had been before.

'They're back all right,' said Julian. 'I wonder where they are. Don't let's drag this clumsy, heavy raft into the boat-house. I don't feel as if I've any strength left in my arms. Let's drag it under a bush and tie it there.'

They thought this a good idea. They pulled the raft up to some thick bushes and tied it firmly to a root that was sticking out of the ground.

Then they made their way to the ruined house, keeping a sharp look-out for Maggie and Dick. There was still no sign of them.

They went in, Timmy first. He didn't growl so they knew it was safe. He led the way to the cellar steps. Then he growled!

'What's up?' said Julian. 'Are they down there, Tim?'

Timmy ran straight down the steps into the cellar room. He growled again, but it was not the fierce growl he always gave when he wanted to warn that enemies or strangers were near. It was an angry, annoyed growl as if something was wrong.

'I expect dear Maggie and Dirty Dick have been down here and found out where our headquarters are!' said Julian, following Timmy down the steps. He switched on his torch.

The beds of heather and bracken were there as they had left them, and their macs and rugs and rucksacks. Nothing seemed to have been disturbed. Julian lighted the candles on the mantlepiece and the dark little underground room came to life at once.

'What's the matter with Timmy?' asked George, coming down into the room. 'He's still growling. Timmy, what's up?'

'I expect he can smell that the others have been down here,' said Dick. 'Look at him sniffing all round. It's quite clear that *someone* has been here.'

'Anyone hungry?' asked Anne. 'I could do with some cake and biscuits.'

'Right,' said Julian, and opened the cupboard where they had put the food they had bought.

There was none there! Except for the crockery and one or two odds and ends that had been in the cupboard before, there was nothing. The bread had gone, the biscuits, the chocolate – everything!

'Blow!' said Julian, angrily. 'Look at that! The beasts! They've taken all our food – every bit. Not even a biscuit left. We were mad not to think they might do that!'

'Clever of them,' said Dick. 'They know we can't stay here long without food. It's a good way of chasing us out. It's too late to go and get any tonight, anyway – and if we go tomorrow for some, they'll do what they have come to do in their own time . . . when we're not here.'

Everyone felt distinctly down in the dumps. They were hungry and tired, and a good meal would have made all the difference. Anne sank down on her bed of heather and sighed.

'I wish I'd left some chocolate in my rucksack,' she said. 'But I didn't leave any there at all. And poor Tim – he's hungry too! Look at him sniffing in the cupboard and looking round at George. Tim, there's nothing for you. The cupboard is bare!'

'Where are those two wretches gone?' suddenly said Julian, fiercely. 'I'll tick them off! I'll tell them what I think of people who come and rifle cupboards and take away all the food.'

'Woof,' said Timmy, in full agreement.

76

Julian went angrily up the stairs. He wondered again where Maggie and Dirty Dick were. He went to the empty doorway and looked out. Then he saw where they were.

Two small tents had been put up under some thickly growing trees! So that's where the two were going to sleep. He debated whether or not to go and tell them what he thought of people who stole food. He decided that he would.

But when he got over to the tents with Timmy, there was no one there! Rugs were laid inside, and there was a primus stove and a kettle and other odds and ends. At the back of one tent was

Timmy came down the stone steps and ran to George

a pile of something, covered by a cloth.

Julian had a good look into each tent, and then went to see if he could find out where Maggie and Dirty Dick had gone. He saw them at last, walking through the trees. They must have gone for an evening stroll, he thought.

They didn't come back to the tents, but sat down by the lake. Julian gave up the thought of tackling them and went back to the others. Timmy was left behind, snuffling about happily.

'They've got tents,' Julian informed the others when he was back in the cellar room again. 'They're obviously staying put till they've got what they came for. They aren't in the tents – they're out by the lake.'

'Where's Timmy?' asked George. 'You shouldn't have left him behind, Ju. They might do something to him.'

'Here he is!' said Julian, as a familiar noise of claws clattering on the ground came to their ears. Timmy came down the stone steps and ran to George.

'He's got something in his mouth!' said George, in surprise. Timmy dropped it into her lap. She gave a yell.

'It's a tin of shortbread! Where did he get it from?'

Julian began to laugh. 'He must have taken it from one of the tents!' he said. 'I saw something covered up with a cloth in one tent – their food, I imagine! Well, well – tit for tat – they took our food and now Timmy is taking theirs!'

'Fair exchange is no robbery,' grinned Dick. 'Serves them right! I say – Tim's gone again!'

He was back in a minute with something large and paper-covered. It was a big cake! The four roared with laughter.

'Timmy! You're a wonder! You really are!'

Timmy was pleased at this praise. Off he went again and brought back a cardboard box in which was a fine pork-pie. The children could hardly believe their eyes.

'It's a miracle!' said Anne. 'Just as I had made up my mind to starve for hours! A pork-pie of all things! Let's have some.'

'Well, I have no second thoughts about it,' said Julian, firmly. 'They took our food and we deserve some of theirs. Good gracious – don't say Tim's gone again.'

He had! He was enjoying himself thoroughly. He arrived this time with a packet of ham, and the children couldn't *imagine* how he had stopped himself from eating some on the way.

'Fancy carrying it in his mouth and not even *tasting* a bit!' said Dick. 'Tim's a better person than I am. I'd just have to have had a lick.'

'I say – we ought to stop him now,' said Julian, as Timmy ran up the steps again, his tail wagging nineteen to the dozen. 'We're getting a bit too much in exchange!'

'Oh, do see what he brings back this time,' begged Anne. 'Then stop him.'

He came back carrying an old flour bag in which something had been packed. Timmy carried it cleverly by the neck so that nothing had fallen out. George undid the bag.

'Home-made scones – and buns,' she said. 'Timmy, you are very very clever, and you shall have a wonderful supper. But you are not to go and take any more things, because we've got enough. See? No more. Lie down and be a good dog and eat your supper.'

Timmy was quite willing. He wolfed ham and scones and a slice of cake, and then he went up into the kitchen, jumped into the sink and lapped the water lying there. He then jumped down and went to the doorway to look out. He barked. Then he growled loudly.

The children rushed up the stone steps at once. Outside, at a safe distance, was Dirty Dick.

'Have you been taking any-

'Grrrr,' said Timmy, so fiercely that the man started back in fright

thing of ours?' he shouted.

'No more than you have been taking of ours!' shouted back Julian. 'Fair exchange, you know, and all that.'

'How dare you go into our tents?' raged the man, his shock of hair making him look very peculiar in the twilight.

'We didn't. The dog fetched and carried for us,' said Julian. 'And don't you come any nearer. He's just longing to fly at you! And I warn you, he'll be on guard tonight, so don't try any funny tricks. He's as strong and savage as a lion.'

'Grrrr,' said Timmy, so fiercely that the man started back in fright. He went off without another word, shaking with anger.

Julian and the others went back to finish a very delicious supper. Timmy went with them--but he planted himself at the top of the cellar steps.

'Not a bad place for him to be tonight,' said Julian. 'I don't trust that couple an inch. We can give him one of our blazers to lie on. I say--this has boiled up into quite an adventure, hasn't it? It seems frightful to think we'll be back at school on Tuesday!'

'We *must* find the loot first!' said Anne. 'We really must. Let's get out that plan again, Ju. Let's make sure that Tall Stone is marked on it.'

They got it out and put it on the table. They bent over it once more.

'Yes--Tall Stone is marked at the end of one of the lines,' said Julian. 'Tock Hill is at the end of the opposite line. Let's get the map and see if there *is* a Tock Hill.'

They got the map, and studied it. Anne suddenly put her finger down on it. 'There it is. On the opposite side of the lake from where we saw the Tall Stone. Tock Hill on one side. Tall Stone on the other. Surely that *means* something.'

'It does, of course,' said Julian. 'It is bearings given to show the whereabouts of the hidden goods. There are four bearings given--Tall Stone. Tock Hill. Chimney. And Steeple.'

'Listen!' said Dick, suddenly. 'LISTEN! *I* know how to read that map. It's easy.'

The others looked at him in surprise and doubt.

'Read it, then,' said Julian. 'Tell us what it all means. I don't believe you can!'

Chapter 18

A Very Exciting Time

'LET'S take all the clues we know,' said Dick, looking excited. 'Two Trees. That's here. Gloomy Water. That's where the hidden stuff must be. *Saucy Jane*. It's a boat that contains the stuff hidden somewhere on Gloomy Water.'

'Go on,' said Julian, as Dick paused to think.

'Maggie is the next clue – well she's here, probably an old friend of Nailer's,' said Dick. 'She knows all the clues too.'

He jabbed his finger at the piece of paper. 'Now for *these* clues. Listen! We saw Tall Stone when we were out on the lake, didn't we? Very well. There must be SOME spot on the lake from where we can see not only Tall Stone, but also Tock Hill, Chimney and Steeple, whatever they are! There must be only one spot from which we can see all those four things at the same time – and *that's* the spot to hunt in for the treasure!'

There was an astonished silence after this. Julian drew a long breath and clapped Dick on the back.

'Of course! What idiots we were not to see it before. The *Saucy Jane* must be somewhere on – or in – the lake at the spot where all four clues are seen at the same time. We've only got to explore and find out!'

'Yes – but don't forget that Maggie and Dirty Dick know what these clues mean too! They'll be there first if they possibly can!' said Dick. 'And what's

more if they get the goods we can't do anything about it. We're not the police! They'll be off and away with their find and disappear completely.'

Everyone began to feel intensely excited. 'I think we'd better set off early tomorrow morning,' said Julian. 'As soon as it's light. Otherwise Maggie and Dick will get in first. I wish to goodness we had an alarm clock.'

'We'll go on the raft, and we'll paddle about till we see Tall Stone again – then we'll keep that in sight till we see Tock Hill, whatever that is,' said Dick. 'And once we've spotted that we'll keep both Tall Stone *and* Tock Hill in sight and paddle round to find out where we can see a steeple – and then a chimney. I should think that would be the one chimney left on Two Trees house! Did you notice there is just one left, sticking up high?'

'Yes, I noticed,' said Anne. 'What a clever way to hide anything, Dick. Nobody could poss-

ibly know what the clues meant unless they knew something of the secret. This is *awfully* exciting!'

They talked about it for some time and then Julian said they really must try and go to sleep or they would never wake up early enough in the morning.

They settled down in their beds of heather and bracken. Timmy lay on Julian's blazer on the top step of the stairs leading down to the cellar room. He seemed to think it was quite a good idea to sleep there that night.

They were all tired and they fell asleep very quickly. Nothing disturbed them in the night. The fox came again and looked into the old house, but Timmy didn't stir. He merely gave a small growl and the fox fled, his bush tail spread behind him.

The morning came and daylight crept in at the burnt-out doorway and windows. Timmy stirred and went to the door. He looked towards the two tents. No one was about there. He went to the cellar steps and clattered down waking Dick and Julian at once.

'What's the time?' said Julian, remembering immediately that he was to wake early. 'Half-past seven. Wake up, everyone! It's daylight. We've heaps to do!'

They washed hurriedly, combed out their hair, cleaned their teeth, and tried to brush down their clothes. Anne got ready some snacks for them – ham, scones and a piece of shortbread each. They all had a drink of water and then they were ready to go.

There was no sign of anyone near the two tents. 'Good,' said Julian. 'We'll be there first!'

They dragged the raft out and got on to it, taking up the paddles. Then off they went, Timmy too, all feeling tremendously excited.

'We'll paddle out to where we think we were last night when Anne caught sight of Tall Stone,' said Julian. So they paddled valiantly, though their arms were stiff with yesterday's paddling and it was really very painful to use the tired muscles all over again!

They paddled out to the middle of the lake and looked for Tall Stone. It didn't seem anywhere to be seen! They strained their eyes for it, but for a long time it was not to be spotted at all. Then Dick gave a cry. 'It's just come into sight. Look, when we passed those tall trees on the bank yonder, Tall Stone came into view. It was behind them before that.'

'Good,' said Julian. 'Now I'm going to stop paddling and keep Tall Stone in sight. If it goes out of sight I'll tell you and you must back-paddle. Dick, can you possibly paddle and look out for something that could be Tock

Hill on the opposite side? I daren't take my eyes off Tall Stone in case it disappears.'

'Right,' said Dick, and paddled while he looked earnestly for Tock Hill.

'Got it!' he said suddenly. 'It must be it! Look, over there – a funny little hill with a pointed top. Julian, can you still see Tall Stone?'

'Yes,' said Julian. 'Keep your eyes on Tock Hill. Now it's up to the girls. George, paddle away and see if you can spot Steeple.'

'I can see it now, already!' said George, and for one moment the boys took their eyes off Tall Stone and Tock Hill and looked

He dropped them into the water, letting out the string as they went down.

where George pointed. They saw the steeple of a faraway church glinting in the morning sun.

'Good, good, good,' said Julian. 'Now Anne – look for Chimney – look down towards the end of the lake where the house is. Can you see its one chimney?'

'Not quite,' said Anne. 'Paddle just a bit to the left – the left, I said, George! Yes – yes, I can see the one chimney. Stop paddling everyone. We're here!'

They stopped paddling but the raft drifted on, and Anne lost the chimney again! They had to paddle back a bit until it came into sight. By that time George had lost her steeple!

At last all four things were in view at once, and the raft seemed to be still and unmoving on the quiet waters of the lake.

'I'm going to drop something to mark the place,' said Julian, still keeping his eyes desperately on Tall Stone. 'George, can you manage to watch Tall Stone and Steeple at the same time? I simply must look what I'm doing for the moment.'

'I'll try,' said George, and fixed her eyes first on Tall Stone, then on Steeple, then on Tall Stone again, hoping and praying that neither would slip out of sight if the raft moved on the water.

Julian was busy. He had taken his torch and his pocket-knife out of his pocket and had tied them together with string. 'I haven't enough string, Dick,' he said. 'You've got some, haven't you?'

Dick had, of course. He put his hand into his pocket, still keeping his eyes on Tock Hill and passed his string over to Julian.

Julian tied it to the end of the string that joined together the knife and torch. Then he dropped them into the water, letting out the string as they went down

They all bent over the edge of the raft and looked down

with their weight. The string slid through his hands. It stopped in a short while and Julian knew that the knife and torch had reached the bed of the lake.

He felt in his pockets again. He knew he had a cork somewhere that he had carved into a horse's head. He found it and tied the end of the string firmly round it. Then he dropped the cork thankfully into the water. It bobbed there, held by the string, which led right down to the knife and torch on the lake-bed below.

'It's done!' he said, with a sigh of relief. 'Take your eyes off everything! I've marked the place now, so we don't need to glue our eyes on the four bearings!'

He told them how he had tied together his knife and torch and dropped them on string to the bottom of the lake, and then had tied a cork to the other end, so

that it would bob and show them the place.

They all looked at it. 'Jolly clever, Ju,' said Dick. 'But once we slide away from this spot, and it would be an easy thing to do, we'd find it jolly difficult to find that cork again! Hadn't we better tie something else to it?'

'I haven't got anything else that will float,' said Julian. 'Have you?'

'I have,' said George, and she handed him a little wooden box. 'I keep the two-penny bits I collect in that,' she said, putting the money into her pocket. 'You can have the box. It will be much easier to see than the cork.'

Julian tied the box to the cork. It was certainly a good deal easier to see! 'Fine!' he said. 'Now we're quite all right. We must be right over the loot!'

They all bent over the edge of the raft and looked down – and they saw a most surprising

sight! Below them, resting on the bottom of the lake, was a boat! It lay there in the shadows of the water, its outline blurred by the ripples the raft made – but quite plainly it was a boat!

'The *Saucy Jane!*' said Julian, peering down, feeling amazed and awed to think that they had read the bearings so correctly that they were actually over the *Saucy Jane* herself! 'The Nailer must have come here with the stolen goods – got out the *Saucy Jane* and rowed her to this spot. He must have taken his bearings very carefully indeed, and then holed the boat so that she sank down with the loot in her. Then I suppose he swam back to shore.'

'Most ingenious,' said Dick. 'Really, he must be a jolly clever fellow. But I say, Julian – how on earth are we going to get the boat up?'

'I can't imagine,' said Julian. 'I simply – can't – imagine! I hadn't thought of that.'

Timmy suddenly began to growl. The four looked up quickly to see why.

They saw a boat coming over the water towards them – the *Merry Meg,* with Maggie and Dirty Dick in it. And the children felt quite certain that both were reading the bearings on their piece of paper in exactly the same way as they themselves had!

They were so engrossed in watching for Tall Stone, Tock Hill, Chimney and Steeple that they took no notice of the children at all. 'I don't think they guess for one moment that we've read the bearings and marked the place,' said Julian. 'How wild they'll be when they find we are right over the place they're looking for! Watch out for trouble!'

81

FA–F

Maggie and Dick Are

Annoyed

In the Moonlight

THEY paddled rapidly away. Dick took a last glance back to make sure that the cork and the box were still bobbing on the water to mark the place where the sunken boat lay. Yes – they were still there.

'It'll be maddening if it's

As soon as Maggie saw the children coming back again, she and Dirty Dick disappeared into their tents

'It won't,' said Julian, looking at the sky. 'The weather's set fine again.'

As soon as Maggie saw the children coming back again, she and Dirty Dick disappeared into their tents. Julian grinned. 'They've heaved a sigh of relief and gone to have a snack,' he said. 'I could do with one myself.'

Everyone felt the same. Paddling was hard work, and the air on the lake was keen-

the cellars beyond, and brought out the food. 'A large toad was looking at it with great interest,' he said, as he brought it back. 'Timmy also looked at the toad with interest – but he's wary of toads by now!'

They took the meal up into the sunshine and enjoyed it. The orangeade was finished so they drank the cold clear water, pumping some vigorously.

'Do you know it's a quarter to

cloudy tonight and the moon doesn't come out,' said George, as they paddled. 'We shouldn't be able to see Tock Hill, Tall Stone and the rest – and we might paddle for ages in the dark without spotting our cork-and-box mark.'

'Don't cross your bridges before you come to them,' said Dick.

'I'm not,' said George. 'I was only just *hoping* that wouldn't happen.'

– quite enough to give anyone a large appetite!

They pushed the raft into its hiding-place again. Then they made their way to the old house. They went down into the cellar room. Timmy growled and sniffed about again.

'I bet Maggie and Dirty Dick have been here, snooping round again,' said George. 'Looking for their pork-pie and ham! Good thing you locked it up, Ju!'

Julian unlocked the door into

three?' said Julian amazed. 'Where has the time gone? In a couple of hours or so it will be dark. Let me see – the moon will be well up about eleven o'clock. That's the time to go, I think.'

'Please don't let's,' said Anne.

'Now you know you don't mean that, Anne,' Julian said. 'You know you'll enjoy it all when the time comes. You couldn't bear to be left out of it! Could you?'

'No. I suppose I couldn't,' said

Anne. 'But I *don't* like Maggie and Dirty Dick!'

'Nor do we,' said Julian, cheerfully. 'That's why we're going to beat them at their own game. We're on the side of the right, and it's worth while running into a bit of danger for that. Now let's see – perhaps we'd better just keep an eye on that couple till it's dark – just in *case* they try any funny tricks – and then we'll have a snooze, if we can, so as to be sure to be lively tonight.'

'There they are!' said Anne. As she spoke Maggie and her companion came out of their tents. They had a few words together and then walked off to the moorland.

'Taking their usual stroll, I suppose,' said Dick. 'Let's have a game of cricket. There's a bit of wood over there for a bat, and I've got a ball in my rucksack.'

'Good idea,' said Julian. 'I still feel a bit chilled from my bathe. Brrrrrr! That water was cold. I don't feel very thrilled at the thought of diving in tonight!'

'I'll do that,' said Dick, at once. 'My turn this time!'

'No. I know exactly where to spot the loot,' said Julian. 'I'll have to go down. But you can come down too, if you like, and help to tie the rope on to it.'

'Right,' said Dick. 'Now look out – I'm going to bowl!'

They enjoyed their game. The sun sank lower and lower, then it disappeared. A cloud came over the sky and darkness came quickly. George looked up at the sky anxiously.

'It's all right,' said Julian. 'It'll clear. Don't you worry!'

Before they went back into the house Julian and Dick slipped down to the boat-house for the coil of rope they would want that night. They found it easily enough and came back, pleased.

It was quite good strong rope, frayed only in one place.

Julian was right about the weather. The sky cleared again in about an hour, and the stars shone crisply. Good!

Julian put Timmy on guard at the doorway. Then he and the others went into the dark cellar-room and lighted a couple of candles. They all snuggled down into their beds of heather.

'I shan't be able to snooze,' complained Anne. 'I feel much too excited.'

'Don't snooze then,' said Dick. 'Just have a rest and wake us up at the right time!'

Anne was the only one who didn't fall into a comfortable doze. She lay awake, thinking of this new adventure of theirs. Some children always had adventures and some didn't. Anne thought it would be much nicer to *read* about adventures than to have them. But then probably the ones who only read about them simply longed to have the adventures themselves! It was all very difficult.

Anne woke the others at ten to eleven. She shook George first, and then the boys. They were all in such a comfortable sleep that it was hard to wake them.

But soon they were up and about, whispering. 'Where's the rope? Good, here it is. Better put on blazers *and* macs. It'll be freezing on the lake. Everyone ready? Now – not a sound!'

Timmy had come to the cellar room as soon as he had heard them stirring. He knew he had to be quiet so he didn't give even one small bark. He was thrilled to find they were going out into the night.

The moon was well up now, and although it was not full, it was very bright. Small clouds swam across the sky, and every

now and again the moon went behind one of them and the world became dark. But that was only for a minute or two, then out it came again, as brilliant as ever.

'Any sign of the others?' whispered Dick. Julian stood at the doorway and looked towards the tents. No – all was quiet there. Still, it would be better if he and the others crept round the side of the house and kept in the shadows.

'We don't want to run any risk of them spotting us now,' whispered Julian, giving his orders. 'Keep out of the moonlight, whatever you do. And see that Tim walks to heel, George.'

Keeping well in the shadows the five crept down to the lakeside. The water gleamed in the moonlight, and a bright moon-path ran all down it, lovely to see. The lake looked very dark and brooding. Anne wished it had a voice of some kind – even the little lap-lap-lap of waves at the edge. But there was none.

They pulled out the raft and threw the coil of rope on to it. Then they clambered on, enjoying its smooth bob-bob-bobbing as they paddled out on the water. They were off!

Timmy was thrilled. He kept licking first one of the four, then another. He loved going out in the night. The moon shone down on the little company and turned every little ripple to silver as the raft bobbed over the water.

'It's a heavenly night,' said Anne, looking round at the silent trees that lined the banks. 'The whole place is so quiet and peaceful.'

An owl immediately hooted very loudly indeed from the trees and Anne jumped violently.

'Now don't start all the owls

The boys twisted it tightly round the top part of the bag

hooting by talking about how quiet everything is,' teased Julian. 'I agree though that it really is a heavenly evening. How calm and mirror-like this lake is. I wonder if it ever produces a wave of any sort! Do you suppose it stays like this even in a storm?'

'It's a queer sort of lake,' said Dick. 'Look out, Timmy – that's my ear. Don't lick it all away. I say – anyone looking out for our four bearings?'

'Well, we know more or less where we've got to paddle the raft to,' said Julian. 'We'll go in that direction and then see if we're spotting the bearings. I'm sure we're going right at the moment.'

They were. George soon saw Tall Stone, and then Tock Hill came into sight. It wasn't long before Steeple was seen too, shining in the moonlight.

'I bet the Nailer came and hid his loot out here on a moonlit night,' said Julian. 'All the bearings can be seen so very clear-

ly – even Tall Stone. We really must find out sometime what it is. It looks like a great stone pointer of some sort, put up in memory of something or somebody.'

'There's One Chimney now,' said Anne. 'We have got them all in view – we should be near our mark.'

'We are!' said Dick, pointing to a little dark bobbing thing nearby. 'The cork and the box. How extremely clever we are! I really have a great admiration for the Five!'

'Idiot!' said Julian. 'Go on, strip now, Dick – we'll do our job straight away. Brrrrrrr! It's cold!'

Both boys stripped quickly, putting their clothes into a neat pile in the middle of the raft. 'Look after them, Anne,' said Julian. 'Got the rope, Dick? Come on, then, in we go. We can't see the boat now, the waters are so dark – but we know it's just below the cork and the box!'

The boys dived in one after the other. Splash! Splash! They were both beautiful divers. The raft rocked as they plunged in and Timmy nearly went in too.

Julian had dived in first. He opened his eyes under the water and found that he could see the sunken boat just below him. With two strong strokes he reached it, and tugged at the waterproof bag there. Dick was beside him almost at once, the rope in his hands. The boys twisted it tightly round the top part of the bag.

Before they could finish the job they had to rise up to the surface to breathe. Dick couldn't hold his breath under water as long as Julian and he was up first, gasping painfully. Then Julian shot up.

The girls knew better than to ask anything just then. They waited anxiously till the boys' breathing grew easier. Julian turned and grinned at them.

'Everything's all right!' he said. 'Now – down we go again!'

Chapter 21
The Sack At Last

DOWN went the boys again and once more the raft jerked violently. The girls peered anxiously over the edge, waiting for them to return.

Julian and Dick were down at the sunken boat in a matter of a second or two. They finished the task of tying the rope to the waterproof bag. Julian gave it a hard jerk, hoping to free it if it were wedged tightly into the boat. He took the rest of the rope length in his hands in order to take it up to the surface.

Then, bursting for breath again, the two boys shot up to the raft, popping out of the water with loud gasps. They climbed on board.

They took a minute to get their breath and then Dick and Julian took the rope together. The girls watched, their hearts beating fast. Now was the test! Would that waterproof sack come up – or not?

The boys pulled strongly but without jerking. The raft slanted and Anne made a grab at the pile of clothes in the middle. Dick fell off into the water again.

He climbed back, spluttering. 'Have to pull more smoothly,' he said. 'I felt the sack give a bit, didn't you?'

Julian nodded. He was shivering with cold, but his eyes were shining with excitement. Anne put a macintosh round his shoulders and one round Dick's too. They never even noticed!

'Now – pull again,' said Julian. 'Steady does it – steady – steady! It's coming! Gosh, it's really coming. Pull, Dick, pull!'

As the heavy bag came up on the end of the rope, the raft slanted again, and the boys pushed themselves back to the other side of the raft, afraid of upsetting everyone into the water. Timmy began to bark excitedly.

'Be quiet, Timmy,' said George at once. She knew how easily sound travels over water, and she was afraid the couple in the tents might hear him.

'It's coming – it's there, look – just below the surface!' said Anne. 'One more pull, boys!'

But it was impossible to pull the heavy bag on board without upsetting the raft. As it was, the girls got very wet when the water splashed over the raft as it jerked and slanted.

'Look – let's paddle back to the shore and let the sack drag behind us.' said Julian, at last. 'We shall only upset the raft. Dress again, Dick, and we'll get back to the old house and open the sack in comfort. I'm so cold now that I can hardly feel my fingers.'

The boys dressed as quickly as they could. They were shivering, and were very glad to take up their paddles and work hard to get the raft back to shore. They soon felt welcome warmth stealing through their bodies, and in ten minutes had stopped shivering. They felt very pleased with themselves indeed.

They looked back at the bulky object following them, dragging along just under the surface. What was in that bag? Excitement crept over all of them again, and the paddles struck through the water at top speed as all the four strained to get back as quickly as possible. Timmy felt the excitement too, and wagged his long tail without ceasing as he stood in the middle of the raft, watching the thing that bobbed along behind them.

They came at last to the end of the lake. Making as little noise

Dick and Julian dragged the waterproof sack out of the water

as possible they dragged the raft under its usual bush. They did not want to leave it out on the bank in case Maggie and Dirty Dick saw that it had been used again, and started wondering.

Dick and Julian dragged the waterproof sack out of the water. They carried it between them as they went cautiously back to the house. It looked a most miserable, grotesque place with its burnt-out roof, doorways and windows – but the children didn't notice its forlorn appearance in the moonlight – they were far too excited!

They walked slowly up the overgrown path between the two broken-down walls, their feet making no sound on the soft mossy ground. They came to the doorway and dragged the bundle into the kitchen.

'Go and light the candles in the cellar room,' said Julian to George. 'I just want to make sure that that couple are not snooping anywhere about.'

George and Anne went to light the candles, flashing their torches before them down the stone steps. Julian and Dick stood at the open doorway, facing the moonlight, listening intently. Not a sound was to be heard, not a shadow moved!

They set Timmy on guard and left him there, dragging the dripping, heavy bundle across the stone floor of the kitchen. They bumped it down the cellar steps – and at last had it before them, ready to be opened!

Julian's fingers fumbled at the knots of the rope. George couldn't bear waiting. She took a pocket-knife and handed it to Julian.

'For goodness' sake, cut the rope!' she said. 'I simply can't wait another moment.'

Julian grinned. He cut the rope – and then he looked to see how to undo the waterproof wrapping.

'I see,' he said. 'It's been folded over and over the goods, and then sewn up to make a kind of bag. It must have kept the loot absolutely waterproof.'

'Buck *up*!' said George. 'I shall tear it open myself in a minute!'

Julian cut the strong stitches that closed the covering. They began to unwrap the bundle. There seemed to be yards and yards of waterproof covering! But at last it was off – and there, in the middle of the mass of waterproof, were scores of little boxes – leather-covered boxes that everyone knew at once were jewel-boxes!

'It *is* jewellery then!' said Anne, and she opened a box. They all exclaimed in wonder.

A magnificent necklace glittered on black velvet. It shone and glinted and sparkled in the candlelight as if it were on fire. Even the two boys gazed without a word. Why – it was fit for a queen!

'It must be that wonderful necklace stolen from the Queen of Fallonia,' said George at last. 'I saw a picture of it in the papers. What diamonds!'

'Oooh – are they *diamonds*!' said Anne, in awe. 'Oh Julian – what a lot of money they must be worth! A hundred pounds, do you think?'

'A hundred thousand pounds more likely, Anne,' said Julian, soberly. 'My word – no wonder the Nailer hid these stolen goods carefully, in such an ingenious place. No wonder Maggie and

A magnificent necklace glittered on black velvet

Dirty Dick were longing to find them. Let's see what else there is.'

Every box contained precious stones of some kind – sapphire bracelets, ruby and diamond rings, a strange and wonderful opal necklace, ear-rings of such enormous diamonds that Anne was quite sure no one would be able to bear the weight of them!

'I would never, never dare to own jewellery like this,' said Anne. 'I should always be afraid of its being stolen. Did it all belong to the Queen of Fallonia?'

'No. Some to a princess who was visiting her,' said Julian. 'These jewels are worth a king's ransom. I just hate the thought of being in charge of them, even for a little while.'

'Well, it's better that we should have them, rather than Maggie or Dirty Dick,' said George. She held a string of diamonds in her hands and let them run through her fingers. How they sparkled! No one could have imagined that they had been at the bottom of a lake for a year or two!

'Now let's see,' said Julian, sitting down on the edge of the table. 'We're due back at school tomorrow afternoon, Tuesday – or is it Tuesday already? It must be past midnight – gosh, yes, it's almost half past two! Would you believe it?'

'I feel as if I'd believe anything,' said Anne, blinking at the glittering treasure on the table.

'We'd better start off fairly early tomorrow,' went on Julian. 'We've got to get these things to the police . . .'

'*Not* to that awful policeman we saw the other day!' said George, in horror.

'Of course not. I think our best course would be to ring up that

How they sparkled!

nice Mr. Gaston and tell him that we've got important news for the police and see which police station he recommends us to go to,' said Julian. 'He might even arrange a car for us, so that we don't need to take this stuff about in buses. I'm not particularly keen on carrying it about with me!'

'Have we got to carry all these boxes?' said George, in dismay.

'No. That would be asking for trouble if anyone spotted them,' said Julian. 'I fear we'll just have to wrap up the jewels in our hankies and stuff them down into the bottom of our rucksacks. We'll leave the boxes here. The police can collect them afterwards if they want to.'

It was all decided. The four divided up the glittering jewellery and wrapped it carefully into four handkerchiefs, one for each of them. They stuffed the hankies into their rucksacks.

'We'd better use them for pillows,' said Dick. 'Then they'll be quite safe.'

'What! These horrid rough

bags!' said Anne. 'Why? Timmy's on guard, isn't he? I'll put mine beside me under the rug but I just won't put my head on it.'

Dick laughed. 'All right, Anne. Timmy won't let any robber through, I'm quite sure. Now – we start off first thing in the morning, do we, Julian?'

'Yes. As soon as we awake,' said Julian. 'We can't have much to eat. There's only a few biscuits and a bit of chocolate left.'

'*I* shan't mind,' said Anne. 'I'm so excited that at the moment I don't feel I'll ever eat anything again!'

'You'll change your mind tomorrow,' said Julian with a laugh. 'Now – to bed, everyone.'

They lay down on their heather and bracken, excited and pleased. What a week-end! And all because Dick and Anne had lost their way and Dick slept in the wrong barn!

'Good-night,' said Julian, yawning. 'I feel very very rich – richer than I'll ever be in my life again. Well – I'll enjoy the feeling while I can!'

Chapter 22
An Exciting Finish

OHHH...

COME ON, HURRY—THEY'RE GETTING AWAY!

THEN IT WAS DIRTY DICK'S TURN!

AAAAAGH! MY ANKLE!

OUGHT WE TO HELP THEM?

WHAT? NO FEAR! FOR ALL WE KNOW HE MAY BE PRETENDING—THOUGH I DON'T THINK SO. THE CHASE IS OVER, ANYWAY, AND THE MORE TROUBLE THOSE TWO ARE IN— MAGGIE'S DOWN AGAIN, LOOK— THE EASIER IT'LL BE FOR THE POLICE TO PICK THEM UP LATER.

NICELY EMBEDDED IN THE MARSH! WELL, PERSONALLY, I DON'T FEEL SORRY FOR EITHER OF THEM. THEY'RE BAD LOTS!

BAD LOTS WE'VE SEEN THE LAST OF, I HOPE. I EXPECT THE POLICE WILL BE PLEASED TO SET EYES ON THEM. WE'LL TELEPHONE FROM THE POST OFFICE IN REEBLES.

IT WAS A GOOD TWO-HOUR WALK—AND YET IT DIDN'T TIRE THEM. THE EXCITEMENT OF THEIR FIND BROUGHT THEM INTO REEBLES AS QUICKLY AS THEY HAD LEFT 'TWO-TREES'...

RIGHT, DICK, YOU RETURN THE GROUND-SHEETS AND RUGS AND SETTLE UP WITH THE OLD MAN— I'LL PHONE MR. GASTON. I EXPECT HE'LL KNOW WHICH POLICE STATION WE SHOULD CONTACT.

RIGHT.

Post Offi

...WHAT! YOU'VE FOUND THE FALLONIA JEWELS? IN YOUR RUCKSACKS NOW, YOU SAY? I CAN'T BELIEVE IT! YOU'RE NOT SPOOFING ME, ARE YOU?

NO, I'M NOT. NOW CAN YOU PUT US IN TOUCH WITH A RELIABLE POLICE OFFICER?

WELL, YES. YOU WANT THE INSPECTOR AT GATHERCOMBE— A FINE MAN. I'LL TELL HIM TO EXPECT US. WAIT THERE AND I'LL PICK YOU UP IN MY CAR. GIVE ME HALF AN HOUR...

THANK YOU. WE'LL LOOK OUT FOR YOU.

WELL, THAT'S ALL FIXED UP. MR. GASTON WILL BE HERE TO COLLECT US IN HALF AN HOUR.

GOOD. I MUST SAY THAT ALTHOUGH IT'S NICE TO HAVE THINGS HAPPENING TO US, IT'S A SORT OF SAFE, COMFORTABLE FEELING WHEN WE HAND OVER TO THE GROWN-UPS. NOW I WANT ONLY ONE THING— BREAKFAST!

BUT IT WAS A BIT LATE FOR BREAKFAST, SO THEY SETTLED FOR A 'BRUNCH' OF SANDWICHES, BUNS, BISCUITS AND GINGER-BEER. THEY FINISHED JUST AS MR. GASTON ARRIVED...

COME ON, EVERYONE—ALL ABOARD FOR THE POLICE STATION!

ON THE WAY JULIAN SHARED THEIR EXTRAORDINARY STORY...

MY, YOU'RE A BUNCH OF PLUCKY KIDS! MY WORD, I WISH YOU WERE MINE!

AT GATHERCOMBE POLICE STATION THEY WERE USHERED INTO THE INSPECTOR'S OFFICE — AND UNPACKED THEIR TREASURE!

WELL, IT'S RATHER A LONG STORY...

MY GOODNESS, YOU'VE GOT THEM! THE VERY JEWELS! AND TO THINK THE POLICE EVERYWHERE HAVE BEEN HUNTING FOR THEM FOR MONTHS ON END! WHERE DID YOU FIND THEM, YOUNGSTERS?

BUT, WITH THE OTHERS' HELP, JULIAN TOLD THE WHOLE STORY, NOT FORGETTING ONE DETAIL. AND THEN HE CAME TO THE PART ABOUT MAGGIE AND DIRTY DICK...

WAIT! WOULD THEY STILL BE THERE? HALF A MINUTE!

THE INSPECTOR PRESSED A BUTTON ON HIS DESK — AND AN OFFICER APPEARED AT THE DOOR...

YES, SIR?

AND NOW — WHAT'S YOUR PROGRAMME?

TELL JOHNS TO TAKE THREE MEN AND DRIVE UP TO GREEN MARSHES, NEAR GLOOMY WATER. HE'S TO PICK UP TWO PEOPLE FLOUNDERING THERE — MAN AND WOMAN. OUR OLD FRIENDS DIRTY DICK AND MAGGIE MARTIN! LOOK SHARP!

WELL — SHAKE! ALL OF YOU! YOU'RE THE KIND OF KIDS WE WANT IN THIS COUNTRY — PLUCKY, SENSIBLE, RESPONSIBLE YOUNGSTERS WHO USE YOUR BRAINS AND NEVER GIVE UP! I'M PROUD TO MEET YOU!

MUSTN'T FORGET YOU, TIMMY! GOOD BOY!

WELL, WE'RE ALL SUPPOSED TO BE BACK AT SCHOOL BY THREE O'CLOCK — BUT I DON'T THINK WE CAN ARRIVE LOOKING LIKE THIS. IS THERE A HOTEL WHERE WE COULD HAVE A BATH AND CLEAN OUR-SELVES UP?

YOU CAN DO THAT HERE — AND THEN WE'LL RUN YOU BACK TO YOUR SCHOOLS IN THE POLICE CAR. WE CAN'T DO TOO MUCH FOR PEOPLE WHO PRODUCE THE FALLONIA JEWELS OUT OF RUCKSACKS, YOU KNOW!

BY HALF PAST TWO THE FRIENDS WERE WASHED AND BRUSHED — AND READY TO GO!

POLICE

YOU'LL BE INTERESTED TO HEAR THAT WE'VE PICKED UP YOUR COUPLE. THE MAN HAD A BROKEN ANKLE, AND THE WOMAN WAS THIGH-DEEP IN THE MARSH. THEY WERE SO FED UP, THEY QUITE WELCOMED THE POLICE!

GOODBYE, NOW. I'M PROUD TO HAVE MET YOU. GOOD LUCK TO YOU, FAMOUS FIVE!

OH, GOOD! THAT'S SETTLED MAGGIE AND DIRTY DICK, THEN!

YES, GOOD LUCK TO YOU, FAMOUS FIVE — AND MAY YOU HAVE MANY MORE ADVENTURES!